A Brush Wit

The Crystal Ball Conundrum

Tyler Rhodes

Copyright © 2023 Tyler Rhodes

Chapter 1

"Thanks for the lift, love. See you at dinnertime."

My wife of just six months smiled as she leaned out of the driver's side window. "Remember, it's your favourite. So don't be late." Charlie puckered up, so I kissed her then stepped back to better soak in her loveliness, something I couldn't stop doing, and never had been able to.

"Like I could forget sausage and mash with onion gravy. I'm salivating already."

"Got your lunch?" Charlie brushed a wayward golden curl from her tanned face and her blue eyes twinkled. It's what first caught my attention, even beyond how stunningly gorgeous she was. So pale they appeared almost icy, they were anything but. Warm, friendly, and utterly arresting. Just like my Charlie. Her green blouse rippled as the air conditioning fought a losing battle with the open window, making her look like a model on a photo shoot. She was, as Young Dave liked to remind me at least twice a day, way out of my league.

"It's all in here with my kit." I hefted the tool bag that contained my prized paintbrushes, various tools, and, of course, my lunch consisting of sandwiches, a bag of beef Hula Hoops—it's gotta be beef—a bottle of water, my flask of milky tea, and a sneaky pork pie. Plus a half pack of Jaffa Cakes, which I was trying, and failing, to ration myself to one a day.

"Why do you lug that silly tool bag around every day?"

"Silly?" I chuckled. "It's family tradition. This was Dad's before he retired from the painting and decorating game, and his dad's before that. It's an antique. Genuine leather. Can't buy them like this now."

"It's covered in paint!" Charlie giggled.

"Yes, but it's antique paint," I said with a wink.

"Tell your Aunty Clem I'm sorry I haven't had a chance to visit while you've been working here, but I'll see her about half twelve. I assume you'll have eaten your lunch by ten, so do you want me to bring you anything? I've got the entire day off work, so I can pop to Greggs if you want?"

"Stop it. Don't tempt me! You know I'm trying to watch my weight."

"Lucas Moran, love of my life, dear, sweet husband who I could never be without, don't you dare start that again."

"What?" I asked, feigning innocence.

"It's infuriating. You eat like a horse, can put away more than any man I have ever known, but you refuse to put on an ounce of fat. Women have murdered husbands over less, you know."

"I've always been this way. Mum said when I was a kid I would eat more than her and Dad combined. Now I'm thirty-two and it's just the same." I shrugged. "Plus, I'm active all day and I go to the gym three times a week."

"Yes, then have three pints with Young Dave afterwards."

"Only on a Friday," I laughed.

"A handsome man with dark, lustrous hair, smouldering brown eyes, slim and fit, has a decent job, and we have a lovely home. It's like a dream."

"Hey, I'm the lucky one. A perfect wife and a perfect life. Right, I better get a move on. You know how Aunty Clem is about people being on time."

"You mean the tea's brewing and she's got out the cake?"

"Don't know what you're talking about," I mumbled, inspecting my paint-splattered work boots and tugging at my painter's whites, although the dungarees were more of a Jackson Pollock than a blank canvas.

"Yeah, as if."

"I'll see you at lunchtime then. Hopefully my van will be ready this afternoon, and Frank promised to drop it off, so that'll be a relief."

"You bet. A Mini is not designed to ferry ladders and long-handled paint rollers. And why on earth do you need so many buckets?"

"For work. Mixing paint, cleaning brushes, that kind of thing."

"Don't let Aunty Clem get you involved in all that magic nonsense she's obsessed with. She should know better at her age."

"What can I tell you? Everyone needs a hobby."

"She nearly blew herself up the other week."

"Don't exaggerate. She just burnt her eyebrows a little. She was making a potion and thought she'd try something different."

"Just be careful. And keep an eye on her. At her age she should be taking it easy."

"She's as fit as a fiddle and likes to keep busy. And it's not just pretend. She can do things," I whispered, glancing back to the large Victorian detached property to make sure she didn't have her bionic ears activated. Aunty Clem could hear you gossip about her from half a mile, but never heard you the first time when you shouted in her face. Selective hearing is what I called it. Being a wily old woman was Aunty Clem's take on the matter.

With a wave, I watched Charlie drive off then smiled. It was a good day to be alive. Damn fantastic, actually. The sun was shining in the quiet town of Rattlingwood in South Shropshire, and it had been for months, this was the last day of painting at Aunty Clem's—which was kind of a relief as she loved to natter and the job had taken twice as long as it should have—and I had a long list of people waiting for work to be done. Meaning, the bank balance was still robust even though I'd refused any payment from my dear, batty old aunty. She'd insisted on at least buying the paint, and made up for it by plying me with enough tea and cake to satisfy the most ardent painter-cum-handyman and his apprentice, Young Dave. Better known as the one that holds the ladder. When he bothered to turn up. Young Dave was not a morning person, which was a shame, as painting in the middle of summer meant early starts so the paint didn't dry before it was out of the tin.

I paused in the luscious garden at the front of the house and admired Aunty Clem's house. She'd lived here for over fifty years now, having survived my uncle and countless confrontations with the family over her being able to manage such a large property alone. But she was strong-willed, tough as old boots, and battled on in her indomitable way, same as she always had.

The freshly painted white upper storey above the red brick ground floor was gleaming in the sunshine, and the dark window frames were offset nicely. It was, even if I did say so myself, a professional paint job. Young Dave had even been let loose with the blue masking tape and a pot of satin for the lower windows and had proven himself, even if he was still rather slow. But better slow and accurate than speedy and sloppy.

The dappled shade from the large beech tree growing at the edge of the low boundary hedge kept the house cool but blocked too much light, and Aunty Clem had promised to see to it years ago, but never had summoned the nerve. I turned at the familiar chatter from the tree and called out, "Hey, little fella," and got an excitable retort from the rare red squirrel in return. He'd been there for years, as familiar as the tree itself.

Picking up my tool bag, I whistled as I walked to the front door, ready for the final day of painting Aunty Clem's living room. The door was on the latch as usual, even though I'd told her a thousand times to keep it locked, as anyone could just walk in. She would laugh and tell me to stop being a silly boy, that this was a nice neighbourhood and all the criminals were down Partridge Way smoking wacky backy. Shropshire might not be a criminal hub, but there are bad sorts everywhere, and even sleepy suburbs have undesirables.

I breathed deeply after I closed the door behind me, leaving it on the latch for Young Dave, if he turned up. Friday's were not his best day of the week, along with the four preceding it. The smell of fresh paint mingled with Rogan Josh—Aunty Clem liked things spicy—and the familiar scent of an old house that had been the same for decades was inviting and comforting. With the cross-breeze from the many open windows, which I suppose negated there being any point locking the front door, it felt cool and as fresh as the new paint. This was just as much a home as any other I'd ever had. I spent a lot of time here growing up, hanging with my aunty and uncle, and adored the familiarity of a house where the furniture, the pictures, even the carpets, were the same as they'd always been.

But the one overriding tang in the air was the acrid smell of Aunty Clem's magic. No matter what Charlie said, I was certain there was some truth behind the many claims of my aunty as to what she could achieve and that she truly was a witch. Not turn you into a frog kind of thing, but there was definitely something just that bit different about her and her group of friends. They got together once a week to supposedly study and practice magic, when it mostly seemed to consist of drinking vats of tea and putting a significant dent in the output of the local cake shop. The owner went to Barbados three times a year thanks to the demand from the local coven.

The entrance hall, an expansive square room larger than many people's houses, was spotless as always. It always reminded me of the foyer of a posh hotel, which made Aunty Clem smile in delight. The gleaming chequered floor was home to various glossy potted plants, and the coat stand groaned under the weight of more coats than any one lady could ever need. The place reserved for umbrellas was stuffed with incongruous broomsticks, but even Aunty laughed when I asked if she could ride one. "Just for fun, my dear," she would giggle when I asked her every week to show me some moves. But it was the winding stairs that were the real star of the show. A deep red carpet runner, polished brass rods, and a broad half landing where you could pause to look out of the magnificent arched window onto the manicured lawns in the expansive garden, Aunty Clem would often just stand there for hours watching the birds.

Chatter from the dining room disturbed my reverie as the door opened and Aunty Clem came bustling out, empty teapot in hand. As always, she was dressed smartly. Today she had chosen a pair of flared blue cotton trousers, and a white blouse that hung off her slender frame like they were bespoke. Her silver hair hung just past her shoulders, and her make-up was impeccable. You'd never know she was in her seventies, and she remained in fine health. Wise blue eyes always gave the impression of knowing more than she should, and it unsettled some people.

"Blimey, you're starting early today," I noted, catching sight of the other coven members in various states of cake eating, tea swilling, bickering, Tarot card reading, or perusing books of spells.

"I told you yesterday that it's a full moon so we were up at the crack of dawn and went into the forest," said Aunty Clem with a scowl then a smile as she somehow managed to pinch both my cheeks whilst holding onto the teapot.

"Ugh, I tried to blank that. You weren't dancing around naked again, were you?" I accused, terrible images flashing in my head.

"It's tradition, and part of the ritual." Aunty winked.

"Weird tradition if you ask me," I muttered, wondering if I could make a break for it before the others caught sight of me.

"The spell wouldn't be as strong otherwise. You should join us."

"No thanks," I shuddered.

"Here, hold this." Aunty Clem thrust the warm teapot into my hands, then shoved me back into the room and declared, "Lucas is here."

"Hi everyone," I said glumly, nodding to the various men and women, both young and old, who constituted the weekly gathering. I turned to a young girl I'd never seen before and asked, "Are you new?"

"Yes," she said, head bowed, her pale face hidden by shiny black hair hanging down to her waist. Hazel eyes peeped through and her lips were the brightest red I'd ever seen.

"Lucas, this is Emily, although she likes to be called Em. Em, this is Lucas, my nephew, and he's the one I was telling you about."

"Nice to meet you," I said, putting the teapot on the table so I could shake hands.

"You too," said Em, gripping my hand firmly but with an almost imperceptible shake. She was nervous.

"Em joined our coven last month, and she's such a wonderful girl. I told you about her, remember?"

"Thank you for having me. I've always wanted to be part of a coven." Em's eyes blazed as she brushed her hair back, her excitement clear.

"And we finally get some new blood," growled Mike, a portly metalhead with more hair than a barbershop floor, tattoos up his neck and all over his arms, and sporting, bizarrely, a Spice Girls T-shirt.

There were murmurs of agreement from the others, causing Em to bow her head again.

"Well, nice to meet you. I better get on. Lots to do today. Enjoy your, er, covening."

"It's not covening, silly," chided Aunty Clem, smiling warmly at her favourite nephew. And her only one. "It's the name of a group, not what we do."

I followed Aunty back out into the entrance hall and handed her the teapot. "She seems nice."

"Oh, she's lovely. A little shy, but she's got strong magic and is a whizz with the Tarot. I'm just going up into the attic to get mine, then I'll make you a nice cuppa and get a fresh cake. I don't know where they put it all."

"Sounds great."

Aunty Clem practically ran up the stairs, only pausing for a second on the half landing before heading to the attic where she kept her collection of rare books, lots of weird things in jars, and other items that constituted her various magical interests.

I retrieved my tool bag and headed into the living room, then checked over the previous day's work with pride. Young Dave had done a good job of the woodwork, sanding between coats like I'd taught him. The ceiling was patch free, the walls the same, but the walls needed one more quick coat this morning then it was just a matter of a few bits and pieces and we were done.

"Help!" Aunty screamed from the hall.

I dropped my thankfully dry roller and rushed out to find Aunty Clem splayed out on the half landing, Tarot cards everywhere. I raced up the stairs two at a time and bent to her.

"What happened? Are you okay?" I could tell by the angle of her arm and the fact she was ashen and sweating badly that she wasn't, but that's what you're supposed to say in such situations, so I said it.

"I... I don't know. I was just coming down and I... I tripped, I suppose. But I didn't slip, I just... Ow, ow, my arm. Is it broken?" Aunty Clem tried to move, but screamed as she shifted position.

"Just stay still. I'll call an ambulance. You just tripped."

"But I never trip. You know me, Lucas, I'm as steady on my feet as ever."

"Accidents happen even to fit people." I pulled out my phone just as the others came rushing from the dining room, concerned and loud.

"Aunty just had a fall—"

"I did not!" she hissed, wincing in pain.

"—so I'm going to call an ambulance. Everyone stay back and give her some room. Make sure she doesn't move until the ambulance arrives."

As I dialled, a boom shook the house and a thunderous riot of glass and who knew what rained down just outside the front door.

"What was that?" I yelled as Aunty Clem screamed.

"Did a bomb go off?" asked Mike.

"Sounded like it," said Shirley, a woman Aunty's age, batting at her silver hair as though it was on fire.

"My room! It came from the attic," Aunty wailed as she hissed in pain through gritted teeth.

The front door banged open and Young Dave staggered in, his already well-worn painter's whites covered in dust and small chunks of rubble.

"What was that?" Young Dave blurted. "I was just admiring my paintwork when the attic window blew out. And half the roof with it. Glass and brick went flying into the tree and then this little guy landed on my head. I think he's concussed." He revealed the red squirrel, now grey thanks to the dust, cradled in his arms. "He might be dead." My apprentice stared at each of us in turn, then his eyes tracked up to where Aunty Clem lay on the landing. "Did it blow you down the stairs?"

"Aunty had a fall, then something happened upstairs," I said.

"Everyone go back into the dining room please," barked Aunty, but it was clear it pained her.

"I don't think that's a good idea. Maybe go out the back into the garden," I suggested. "There might be another bomb. Young Dave, drop the squirrel and come up here to protect Aunty. I'll go out front and see what the damage is then call an ambulance. Maybe the police too."

"No police," wheezed Aunty Clem. "It might be, er, one of my potions. Might have got the ingredients wrong. Sometimes they're volatile and bubble over."

"Aunty, that wasn't bubbling over. It blew out the attic. It might be a gas leak, or anything."

"There's no gas up there. It's all on the ground floor."

"Or an electrical fault."

"No, it'll be the potions, I'm sure. No police. I don't want them snooping. But be a dear and call the ambulance. I think my arm's sprained."

"It's more than a sprain. Do not move," I warned. I went downstairs, took the comatose squirrel from Young Dave, then whispered to him, "Just keep her company and make sure she doesn't get sleepy. She might have hit her head." Young Dave nodded, then did as I asked while I handed the squirrel to Em, who smiled at me then followed the others out into the garden.

Stressed about Aunty, concerned about explosives and what she'd been up to in the attic, I popped my head out of the front door and gasped as another explosion rocked the house. A deep boom that thundered up and down the street, echoing off the houses. Brick, mortar, timber, and glass littered the front garden as loose tiles slid from the roof. The tree was shredded, and several branches lay across Aunty's prized roses, which were flattened. I risked it and raced along the path to the gate and stared back up at the house. The entire attic was blown out. The window and most of the frame were gone, slates above were missing or cracked, revealing the roof beams, and smoke billowed from the room.

Did we need the fire brigade too? Most likely.

Someone inside the house screamed, or maybe from the garden, then everyone came rushing through the front door, shouting incoherently, panicked. Shirley and Miranda were crying, Em was even paler than ever, and Mike was red and agitated.

"Sylvester's been killed," wheezed Mike, sweating and flustered.

"What? Don't be daft."

"He has. He's dead. He's more than dead, he's super dead. So gross."

I stared at the others, unable to process such grave news. They nodded mutely as they sobbed.

"What is happening?" I sighed, then called the police to report that Sylvester was "super" dead, my Aunty Clem needed an ambulance, and I supposed I'd better call the fire brigade. Maybe the bomb squad.

There was no way I was going to finish the paint job today   now.

Chapter 2

Everyone had been waiting in the entrance hall, in various states of either agitation, indifference, downright fear, or confusion. I couldn't even begin to figure out what was happening beyond that Aunty had tripped, and she'd most likely done something in the attic. But she insisted she hadn't tripped, and now there was a dead body in the garden. I'd gone outside to check, because I simply couldn't believe it was true, but sure enough the once smart appearance of Sylvester, the suited and booted accountant who had been with Aunty ever since she first set up her coven nigh on five years ago, was now anything but a picture of bland precision.

A dark pool had spread around his body where he lay on the neatly clipped lawn surrounded by a traditional English country garden in full bloom. Bees buzzed, birds sang, but flies were beginning to gather and I beat a hasty retreat into the house through the wide back door that led into the dated but spotless kitchen. As I returned to the others, I couldn't get the picture of Sylvester, a ragged wound in his side, out of my head.

"Was it utterly gruesome?" asked Young Dave with rather too much excitement.

"Quiet," I warned, glancing at the others. I pulled Young Dave close and whispered, "One of them must have done it, so watch yourself."

Young Dave's eyes widened and his already pale skin blanched as he cast nervous, suspicious looks at the others, then said, "You think one of Clem's friends is a murderer?"

"What do you think? The attic blew out, then they all go into the garden, and now Sylvester looks like he got hit by a wrecking ball. What can even do that?"

"I'm going to go look. It can't really be a big hole." I reached out to stop him, but Young Dave rushed towards the kitchen, rubbing at his mass of short, bleached-blond hair, ducking to get through the doorway.

I studied the various characters that constituted this peculiar weekly gathering, once again marvelling at the strange group. Em, the new girl, was clutching the squirrel in her arms. Every now and then she sobbed and her shoulders trembled.

Shirley was over by a large potted palm, wringing her hands nervously, rubbing at her eyes with a handkerchief she kept stuffed up her pink cardigan's sleeve. Her white hair was a mess as she tousled it repeatedly, ruining the weekly tight curls she had done without fail.

Mike was up with Aunty Clem, squatting despite his considerable meaty girth, his Spice Girls tee riding high above his faded, ripped jeans. But he was smiling, and chatting away to Aunty to keep her mind off things, and he had always had this gift. Once people got over his initial appearance of tattoos, numerous skull rings, and unruly long brown hair, they warmed to him as he was friendly, always smiling, and his brown eyes and crow's feet gave the impression he was constantly amused.

Last was Miranda, a woman I had never taken to, but that didn't mean she went around blowing up attics and murdering accountants. Early forties, she was a stay-at-home mum who was constantly running around after her two kids. Usually frazzled from not enough sleep, she still maintained an air of respectability, wearing tight designer jeans, tops that were too figure-hugging, and more make-up than was strictly necessary. I didn't understand the craze for thick fake eyelashes, but I was a painter and handyman, not a fashion expert.

There was just something about her. The way she put on airs and graces, acted posh just because she lived in a big house with an overpaid husband and two rude, demanding children Everyone knew she was brought up in a two-up two-down like most people around here, and that good fortune in life didn't suddenly make you better than anyone else. Miranda's make-up was smeared, her loose, bouncy auburn hair was now limp from her tugging at it repeatedly, and yet she wasn't watching the others, didn't seem afraid, just distraught.

It still, after five years, seemed incongruous that these people found common ground and got together every Friday to practice what they called their art, but was often little more than a tea and cake-fest followed by Tarot reading. Sometimes there was a crystal ball, other times they pored over books on magic, and sometimes they made potions or locked themselves away for hours in the attic. Aunty Clem insisted each of them knew real magic, that they were all improving with their various gifts, and that it was a true coven, but she'd never shown me proof and I put it down to one of those things. I'd only met them a handful of times over the years, as Friday evenings were reserved for the gym and pub with Young Dave after work then home, but to be fair, and much to my surprise, as the coven filled with members they'd all stuck around and seemed to enjoy their time together.

"Can you hold him?" mumbled Em through her hair as she thrust the comatose squirrel at me.

"Um, sure. You okay? Er, need a hug or something?"

Em took a step back and said, "No, I'm good," as she handed me the poor creature.

I studied the limp red squirrel, surprised by its warmth and size, having always thought of it as larger. It was surprisingly delicate, with a body no bigger than a kitten, but the bushy tail made up for it and more than doubled its size. "Think he'll be okay?" I asked.

"We should call a vet."

"Yes, you're right. I didn't think."

"Because of the murder," gulped Em, glancing at the kitchen door.

"Yes. Um, no. It wasn't a murder, surely? Must have been the attic debris. How are you holding up? It's a lot to take in."

"I... I can't believe it. This is only my fourth time here, and they all seem so nice."

"So you're into magic then? Can you do real spells?"

Em's head shot up and she parted her hair, fixing her eyes on me. As her cheeks reddened, she said, "Yes, of course. You don't believe?"

"It doesn't matter if I do or not. But Aunty's never shown me anything. She's always said it's for the best, and she's still learning, but you know." I shrugged.

"I've always been gifted, and some of the others are too. Clem's quite adept, especially only having begun again in her later years."

I chuckled. "She's feisty though, and she won't be happy having to take it easy because of her fall. Even though she insists she didn't trip."

"I'll come watch her as much as I can. I can read some of her books if they're still there."

"Damn, her collection in the attic. I should check. But maybe later. You hear that? I think it's a siren." With a nod to Em, I went outside, still cradling the squirrel. He stirred as we hit the fresh air, then opened an eye and looked at me before going limp again. He was covered in what seemed to be yellow and purple dust—what I could only assume was powder from the various chemicals Aunty used for her potions.

"Just don't turn into a frog," I told him, then jumped back, startled, when he suddenly went rigid, his eyes opened, and he sprang from my arms, chattering as he raced across the front garden and up into the beech tree. He sat on his favourite branch and called noisily as I watched a police car grind to a halt. Two officers came up the path, talking into walkie-talkies clipped to their lapels.

I explained to the officers what had happened, and they took it in without comment until I mentioned the hole in Sylvester.

"A hole?" scoffed the burly older officer. "You mean a bullet wound?"

"No," I snapped, not liking his attitude. "I mean a wound I bet you can see clean through. Well, you could if he was standing. Or maybe more like a chunk missing. Ugh, do you really need me to explain?"

"And what do you imagine happened?" he asked, stifling a smirk as he nudged the young officer beside him who seemed more confused them amused.

"What? How would I know? It might be pirates for all I know."

"Oh yes, we've got another pirate infestation and they're running amok. We have parrots everywhere, and guys with eye patches waving their curved swords and following treasure maps."

"Not funny, Pete," said the young lad, shaking his head.

"Officer Merryweather, I was just having some banter with this gentleman. The decorator."

"I'm not just the decorator. I told you, she's my aunty. I come here all the time, and I don't think you're taking this seriously."

"Oh, I'm taking it seriously, sir. Just trying to lighten the mood. Don't worry, we'll have this sorted soon enough. The detectives are on their way, and this will be cleared up in no time."

Weirded out by the strange humour, I showed them inside where they checked on Aunty. They told her to stay still and the ambulance was on its way, then left Mike with her while I showed them the garden, reminding everyone not to leave the premises.

"See, told you it was gruesome," I said, ashamed of myself for sounding smug when we were talking about poor Sylvester.

"I stand corrected, sir. It is indeed terrible."

"I think I'm going to be sick," said officer Merryweather as he turned away and made a weird noise.

At that moment, more police arrived, and then the detectives, and soon I was bombarded with questions and had to battle my way back inside to check on Aunty. The paramedics and the fire brigade had arrived, so while Aunty was checked over then put on a stretcher and taken outside, the firemen trundled upstairs to inspect the attic.

I was told I couldn't go with Aunty in the ambulance, but would be required for questioning, and there followed a cacophonous nightmare as the detectives tried to get some sense out of everyone whilst trying not to disturb what could well be multiple crime scenes. With firemen everywhere, officers milling about, and detectives trying to get everyone's movements locked down, it took a while before they managed to organise transport. After those that needed to made phone calls to explain where they were, we were taken to the police station. Charlie said she'd go to the hospital, and I promised to call her the moment this was finished with.

The detectives were kind, patient, and understanding. But very thorough. I went over and over the sequence of events, trying my best to recall everything as it had happened. But you don't, do you? You just do things without taking note of where everyone is or what they are doing, just a general idea of what's going on around you. After Aunty's fall, it was all a blur. Who was where when the attic exploded? Was everyone downstairs? They were, I was sure of that much. But then the others were in the garden when the second blast came, so I had no idea what happened out there.

The detectives thanked me for my patience and told me I could go. After giving my details, I found myself outside the police station watching people go about their everyday lives. Shopping, strolling, smiling, oblivious to the horrors some of us had just experienced. It felt like a dream. Exploding attics, bodies in your aunty's garden? These things didn't really happen, it was just stories on the news. Now it wasn't remote, it was real, and I had to go and make sure Aunty Clem was okay and coping with what for her was most shocking of all. She was hurt, her prized attic was most likely destroyed, and one of her friends had died in her own garden.

The hospital was only a ten minute walk from the centre of town so I dashed over, concerned how Aunty was faring, hating the thought of her being in a strange bed rather than her own at home. She'd never been sick in her life as far as I could recall. Never had to see the doctor, made sure to get her annual flu jab and Covid vaccinations, and even when she caught Covid she did her usual thing and worked it off in the garden and was right as rain in a week.

After the receptionist eventually located Aunty, I spent half an hour getting lost in corridors that looked identical, until finally I was on the right ward and spied Charlie at the foot of one of half a dozen beds in a bustling room full of doctors and nurses doing the rounds.

"Hey." I smiled at Charlie as she moved aside to let the doctor and nurses leave Aunty's bedside.

"Hey." Charlie smiled in sympathy and said, "You look awful. You okay? How did it go?"

"I'll tell you later. But I'm okay. How's Aunty Clem?"

"Doctor," said Charlie, putting a hand to the young, harried-looking man, "could you explain to my husband how Clem is?"

"Yes, of course. It's a clean break of the radius, so she mustn't use her arm for a few weeks. We'll get a cast on it later today, she'll have a sling, and mustn't get it wet, but apart from that she's very resilient. A few bruises, but no other broken bones, and she's thinking straight and her hips are fine, which is usually the first to break in falls down stairs."

"Wow, that's great. Can she go home?"

"Tomorrow. We'll keep her in overnight for observation, but as long as she doesn't deteriorate, she can go home tomorrow after I do my rounds."

"That's great. Thank you, doc," I said, my heart sinking when I looked at Aunty in the hospital bed, wearing a green gown rather than her smart clothes. She suddenly looked very old, and very frail.

The doctor caught my sigh and said, "Don't worry. She had a shock, but she's fit and healthy, so whatever she's been doing make sure she does more of it. Can someone stay with her for at least a few days to ensure she's okay? I'd hate to have to keep her in hospital on a ward. Best place is home for her," he said so Aunty could hear.

She smiled weakly and asked, "Can I go home now? Did they find out what happened to dear Sylvester?"

"I don't know, Aunty. They didn't tell me. But don't worry, you'll be home tomorrow and I'll stay with you."

"So will I," said Charlie.

"You sure?" I asked.

"Of course. Clem's family, and we do right by family. We'll look after you."

"Thank you both. My, what a day. How is the attic?"

"We haven't looked yet."

"Sorry, I have to complete my rounds," said the doctor, then left us alone. Nurses trailed after him, asking a barrage of questions.

Charlie and I took either side of the bed and I said, "Thanks for coming to be with Aunty Clem."

"Of course. I came the moment you called."

"The police asked me so many questions," said Aunty, wincing as she tried to sit more upright.

"Me too. It was exhausting. What a morning. What did they ask you?"

"About the fall, and the attic, and poor Sylvester. I told them what I could, but it happened so fast. Is he really dead? Truly?"

"I'm afraid so. Aunty, what happened in the attic? Why didn't you want the police involved?"

"What's this?" asked Charlie, eyebrows raised.

"I just didn't want them snooping," snapped Aunty. "Sorry, I'm not cross with you two. Lucas, you have been such a good lad, and you kept everyone from going loopy after the, er, incident in the attic. Thank you."

"You're welcome. So, the attic?"

"I know you don't believe, but there really is magic. The attic has some very potent items, and my spellbook. I've been working on it for years, and I didn't want it taken by the police for evidence. Make sure you find it and keep it safe."

"Evidence of what?"

"Oh, nothing, just the usual spells and whatnot. But there are lots of other important books, and my cards, and my crystal ball collection. Even my wand."

"You have a wand?" asked Charlie, catching my eye and shaking her head in bemusement.

"I saw that! You two should let me show you a few things when we get home. It's time."

"Time for what?"

"For you to become believers."

"Okay, I think you should rest up now. Charlie and I will go back to the house to check everything's okay. I'll make sure the place is secure, and see about getting the attic fixed. Better call the insurance company, I suppose."

"No, don't do that! I'll pay for the damage," said Aunty, trying to sit up but wincing then slumping back into the pillows.

"Let's just wait until tomorrow, then. I'm sure the place is still full of investigators or whoever they get when things like this happen."

"Crime scene investigators," said Charlie. "And are we even allowed back there?"

"Of course you are. It's my house. My home."

"But they need to do forensics and make sure it's safe. The attic might explode again," I protested.

"It won't. Must have just been a silly potion gone wrong. You know they sometimes don't work out as planned. That's the fun of being a witch."

"You just rest. Leave it to me and Charlie. I'll come and see you this evening. But try to get some sleep. It's been a big shock and you need to rest."

"I am tired." Aunty stifled a yawn.

With a nod to each other, Charlie and I left her and battled our way out of the hospital. They never used to be this busy, did they? How on earth did they cope with such chaos?

Chapter 3

It was almost one o'clock when we made it back to Aunty Clem's. I'd half-expected to be locked up overnight and interrogated under a swinging light, subject to the full good cop, bad cop routine, but it had been friendly enough, if exhausting. I wondered how the others were faring, as, obviously, one of them was a stone-cold killer. But how? And why?

"You sure you're up for this?" asked Charlie as she turned off the engine.

"Course. I figured I may as well finish the living room."

"Very funny," laughed Charlie, then her smile faltered as I didn't join in. "You aren't serious?"

"Why not? It'll be a nice surprise for Aunty Clem when she gets out tomorrow. Make her feel less freaked out."

"Lucas, there was a bomb, or whatever it was, in the attic. What's she been doing up there? Can we even go up to take a look?"

"I expect so. There's nobody around, is there?"

"And what's all that about?" Charlie scowled. "Where are the crime scene investigators? The forensics? People in white hazmat suits? What's happening?"

"No idea," I shrugged, then got out of the Mini and stared up at the attic.

Charlie joined me and stifled a few choice swear words, opting instead for a, "Wow! She really does keep explosives up there. I can see the roof beams. Think it's safe?"

"Maybe. I guess it hasn't done it again. But Aunty was acting weird, right? She told me she didn't want the police involved, and she was hardly concerned. I know this magic business is just harmless fun, but the others in her group should know better than to encourage her."

"It's just a way to let off some steam. An interest. People like the esoteric, the paranormal. Gives them something fun to do. They collect books, chase down rare Tarot cards, and it means they've made friends. It's a fad, like she used to be obsessed about roses."

"Yeah, and look at them now." We turned to examine the flattened rose bushes in the border, and once again I was amazed how much damage the explosion had caused. Glass, wood, slate, and even a few still-intact specimen jars littered the path and were strewn across the lawn and mixed up with the shrubs. Even the tree was splattered in various powders I dared not investigate too closely in case I mixed things up that should never be mixed up. The base was thick with paraphernalia that must have hit the branches then dropped. I even spied a Tarot card with a picture of the Grim Reaper, and almost bent to retrieve it then shuddered and thought better of it. "I wonder what really happened?"

"It was an accident like Clem says," said Charlie.

"Bit of a mad coincidence if it was. But she tripped, and that was a coincidence too, right?"

"Maybe she fell when the attic blew out."

"No, I was there, and she was in a heap halfway down and screaming in pain, then the front of the house was torn out."

"Don't exaggerate. It's not that bad. A few slates, repair the joists, a new window, and it'll be as good as new."

"As long as the room's still intact," I griped.

A red blur shot past our legs, then the squirrel paused at the front door and began chattering.

"Oh, did I mention the squirrel?"

"No, you did not! What about it?"

I explained what happened, and Charlie, always a sucker for an injured animal, almost burst into tears. "The poor thing. He fell from the tree?"

"I guess so. And he was covered in powder, and kept sneezing. But then he seemed fine and just ran off. What's he up to now, though?"

"It's like he wants to go inside."

"Aunty will have a fit if I let a squirrel in the house. Come on, let's go see what the police and fire brigade have done. Maybe there will be crime scene tape."

"What are you looking so happy about?" asked Charlie, studying me closely.

"I'm not happy. I'm worried about Aunty, but you have to admit, this is kind of exciting. Not in a good way," I added hurriedly. "In a horrible, nasty, concerning way. But at least Clem's alive and will get better, and she still has a house to come home to."

"You seemed happy."

"Love, it's been a weird morning and then some. But you know me, I'm a positive bloke." I smiled, not knowing what else to say.

With no tape warning us not to enter, and no sign of anyone else, I opened the door with my key—thankfully the latch had been put down—and we went inside. The squirrel darted between our legs and ran to the bottom of the stairs, then sat on its haunches, watching us.

"What is with that squirrel?" I asked.

"Maybe he's still sick." Charlie squatted, then for some reason began talking like she was communicating with a baby. "Hey little fella, you feeling icky? Wanna cuddle?"

"What are you doing? What's wrong with your voice? It's a squirrel, not a simpleton."

"I'm being calming," she said, scowling at me then smiling at the squirrel. "What you doing inside, eh? You feeling lonely?"

The squirrel hopped down the step, then raced forward before halting halfway to us. He cocked his head and looked from Charlie to me, then back again. With his tail twitching, he spun, before resuming his perch on the step.

"He's keen, that's for sure."

"I think he just wants to be left alone," said Charlie. "Is that right, little guy? You want some peace?"

"He probably wants his tree cleaned," I chuckled. "And for the glass to be gone."

"I'll do it in a while, okay, Harlow?"

"Harlow? Where did that come from?"

Charlie beamed at Harlow, then smiled at me, suddenly coy. "Not sure. But he looks like a Harlow, don't you think?"

I studied the twitchy squirrel, currently using his cute little paws to rub at his face, eyes never leaving us, and admitted, "Yeah. I don't know why, but he does look like a Harlow."

At his name, Harlow's head lifted and he chattered away to us. Then he raced from the house out into the front garden.

"I think he likes the name," said Charlie.

"Somehow, I think you're right."

I noted the endless mugs washed up and draining on the sink—the emergency services had clearly worked up a thirst, but at least they'd washed up afterwards, even the teapot and mugs from Aunty's coven. But were they allowed to do that? Guess it was the least of our worries at the moment.

I unlocked the back door using the key always in the lock on the inside, then headed towards the scene of the crime. When I realised Charlie wasn't beside me, I turned to find her at the door, face a mask of concern.

"What's wrong?" I called back.

"Is it horrid?"

I glanced at the lawn, then shook my head. "No, the corpse has gone. They must have taken it."

"How can you talk like that? Words like corpse, and it? *It* was that accountant, Sylvester, not a thing."

"Sorry, I forget I'm a civilian sometimes." I wandered back and took Charlie's hand, then we both walked over to the stained grass, mindful of where we stood, rather confused by the whole matter.

"Where are the forensics people? What's going on? This isn't how they normally do things, is it? The place should be teeming."

"Guess everyone's on lunch break," I shrugged. "Or they found what they wanted and left."

"Is that a thing? Would it happen so fast?"

"Pretty fast for murders. But not this fast, no."

"Sorry about earlier," said Charlie, squeezing my hand.

"Sorry for what?"

"Telling you off for calling Sylvester a corpse. I forget you have probably seen much worse."

"This pales in comparison, trust me. It's why I left. I should never have joined, but it seemed like the right thing to do at the time. And to be fair, I did have some amazing times with the lads. But wielding a paintbrush rather than a weapon is much less stressful. Usually." I stared at the bloodstained grass, forcing down memories of the things I'd seen in parched lands. The things I'd done. It may have only been a few years, but those years were the ones I recalled in every minute, gut-wrenching detail when it should have been the happy times I remembered with the most clarity.

"Lucas, I'm so sorry."

"Don't be. It's in the past, and it made me the man I am today. So if I act a little cold or callous, I apologise. Blood and all kinds of nasty stuff doesn't phase me, but I know it should. I'm just not squeamish, and never have been. Probably why I joined."

"Liar!" Charlie slapped me playfully on the arm. "You joined the army so you didn't have to work for your dad. Then when he retired you took up the mantle."

"The roller, you mean?" I laughed, hugging Charlie and kissing her.

"What was that for, you daft lump?"

"Because I love you, and you are my salvation. I don't deserve you."

"True. I'm way out of your league."

"Have you been talking to Young Dave again?"

"He might have reminded me how amazing I am," giggled Charlie.

"You are. Amazing, wonderful, and my wife."

"And you're my incredible husband. We're both very lucky."

"Certainly much luckier than poor Sylvester "

I let go of Charlie and began to walk around the garden. Studying shrubs and herbaceous perennials, checking the roses, and trying not to get too sidetracked by the sheer beauty, but to inspect things with as professional an eye as I could muster. One thing about being a painter is you have to have an eye for detail. It's what sets you above the competition.

"What are you doing?"

"I'm not sure. But somebody's got to do something."

"Oh, you're looking for clues, aren't you?" teased Charlie.

"Maybe. I hadn't thought about it like that. Just seeing if anything is off. A man died and had a terrible wound. Only time I've ever seen that happen was when... Well, let's just say it's not an easy thing to accomplish and involves some heavy fire-power, of which there was none. Nobody heard a gun or shotgun, and there's no rubble from the attic as that all blew out the front, so I'm stumped."

"And they were all out here? The coven?"

"Apparently. That's what they said. But they were split up and wandering around checking things out while they waited in case the house exploded. I wonder what the police are doing with them?"

"And how poor Young Dave is. He wasn't here then, right?"

"No, he came after the first explosion, with Harlow in his arms. Everyone else was already outside."

"Could Young Dave have done it, then raced back around the front and come in with Harlow?"

"Well, yeah, I guess. But it's Young Dave we're talking about here. He freaks out if he crushes a snail."

"So do you."

"True," I admitted.

"But I think we can rule Young Dave out. So that means it was one of the others. Who are they again?"

I explained who was here, then said, "But it's a bit far-fetched. They aren't the type to murder accountants."

"Really? You of all people should know anyone is capable of it."

"You're right," I conceded. "Given the right conditions and training. But we have a shy young girl, although she is new to the group, an elderly woman, a preening posh wannabe, and Mike the metalhead."

"Maybe Mike's into death metal."

"I'm partial to it myself. Doesn't make me a killer. At least, not anymore. Even if it was one of them, how did they do it?"

"No idea. That's for the police to find out. We need to worry about Clem and the fact there might have been a murderer in her home just waiting for the opportunity to strike."

"Let's go back inside. And we need to call the station, find out what's going on here. We've most likely contaminated a crime scene."

"Then they should have put some of their silly tape up to stop us," pouted Charlie.

"They should. I wonder why they didn't? Maybe I'll call now." I dialled the number the detectives had given me and, amazingly, DI Durham answered on the second ring. I explained where we were and what my concerns were, but he said there was nothing to worry about and everything had already been taken care of. By that, he said the forensics had been and gone, everything had been photographed, and he and his partner had checked over the scene in the few hours I was waiting to be questioned at the station. Officers had double-checked afterwards—there was nothing to be found.

I asked about the others, and was told they were still in for questioning, apart from Young Dave who had been released not long after me. Was this normal, I wondered, to let people return to a crime scene so quickly? He explained that things were different these days, and with all the new technology it never took long to investigate. And besides, it wasn't as if they had to be hunting around for clues. It was obvious the explosion in the attic was because Aunty was mixing dangerous chemicals, and the death was a mystery, yes, but there were no weapons in the garden, or the neighbours', and it would have to be something large to have caused such damage.

Then how did it happen? I wondered. I was told, rather tersely, that the moment they found that out, I'd be one of the first to know. But it was obviously because of the attic. With that, DI Durham hung up.

"Well, that was pointless," I huffed. "I'm assuming you heard that?"

"You had it on speaker, so yes." Charlie frowned, then chewed at her lip like always when deep in thought. "Does this seem utterly unprofessional to you? I mean, someone died, was potentially murdered. And shouldn't they get the bomb squad in?"

"You heard the DI. He said the explosion was Aunty Clem's fault and the investigation into Sylvester is ongoing. How mad is this?"

I was at a loss. What were we meant to do now? Just pretend like it never happened? I took another glance at the garden and something caught my eye, so I wandered over to a shaded patch underneath a large green acer and bent to the dry ground. The earth was coated in red dust, and further around the tree a green patch of something with sparkly bits in it. I got onto all fours and sniffed, then thought better of it in case it was poisonous, and stood hurriedly.

"What is it?" called Charlie.

"I'm not sure, but they sure missed something. Come look."

Charlie hurried over, then her eyes widened. "Think it's from a weapon? Or is it the same as from the attic?"

"I think it's from the attic. Or maybe they were all making potions out here. They do if the weather's nice, apparently. Come to think of it, I see this stuff everywhere. Never thought anything of it. I assumed it was something to do with the garden. Like extra nutrients or something. Aunty Clem is forever sprinkling organic this and nitrogen that around everywhere."

"Maybe that's what it is. And anyway, you can't kill a man with powder."

"No, but when you combine them you can blow up an attic. Could be the exact same stuff."

"Could be. Let's get inside to the cool. It's so hot out here."

"I'm burning up," I agreed.

"That's because you still have your overalls on." Charlie giggled as she pointed.

I looked down at my well-worn white dungarees, noted the new stains of orange, red, green, and gold, mostly likely picked up from Harlow the squirrel, or when I went out front after the attic incident, and hoped I wasn't contagious. No point worrying about it now, but I did give my hands a good scrub in the kitchen sink.

As we went back into the entrance hall, there was a knock at the door so I peered through the peephole, suddenly nervous. Maybe killers knocked these days. Easiest way to get inside is to be let in.

"It's just Young Dave," I told Charlie, who was hiding behind a potted fern. "You know I can see you, right?" I laughed.

"No, you can't," insisted Charlie, smiling and standing, eyes downcast.

I opened the door and Young Dave blustered in, cracked his head on the frame, and squealed as he staggered over to the stairs and sank onto a step.

"What a morning. I thought they were going to lock me up and make me spend the night. Man, those detectives are mean."

"They were nice to me," I said smugly.

"Yeah, but they knew you didn't do it as you and Clem are the only ones with an alibi."

"True. So, they gave you the full works, eh?"

"Not really," shrugged Young Dave as he smiled sheepishly then rubbed at his bleached hair that made him look like a football player from the early eighties. All he needed was a perm and he could probably play for Liverpool. "They just kept asking the same questions, and I told them all I knew, which wasn't much. So, what's been happening? You been upstairs yet?"

"Not yet."

"Oh, hi Charlie. You missed the excitement."

"So it seems. Are you alright? You look exhausted."

"Ha, yeah, I'm okay. Bit freaked out if I'm honest. What with bits of house falling on me, squirrels landing on me, and dead dudes in the garden. And poor Clem. Is she alright? What's the news?"

"She's got a broken arm and is staying in hospital overnight, but she should be okay. We'll stay a few nights with her to ensure she's on the mend."

"Cool, that's good to hear. I like her. Glad it wasn't her that got offed. Who'd you reckon did it then?" Young Dave's eyes gleamed as he stared at the kitchen door, as if he could see through walls and the body was still there.

"No idea. Or how. And apparently forensics and what have you have already been and gone. We were just saying it seems weird."

"They have all this tech now. They just record everything and look it over at their leisure," he shrugged. "And mostly, they'll be focused on the autopsy. That'll be key to finding out what killed the guy. Apart from the big hole, of course."

"Of course," I said, rolling my eyes at Charlie.

"Let's go into the living room. I don't know about everyone else," I said, "but I could do with putting my feet up for five. I'm beat. And we've missed lunch."

With my head reeling, and a sudden lethargy taking me over, we entered the living room and pulled the dust sheets off the sofa, each of us sighing as we sank into the soft, cream leather four-seater.

"Walls look nice," said Young Dave.

"And the ceiling."

"Good job on the baseboards, right?" he beamed.

"Don't you dare!" I warned. "I've told you over and over about that."

"Don't know what you mean," he chuckled.

"We say skirting boards. Always have and always will. This is why I keep telling you to stop watching American home improvement shows. You keep confusing me. I mean, who says trim? What does that even mean? It's skirting and picture rail and dado."

"I'm just joking around with you. The skirting does look ace, right?" Young Dave winked at me, struggling to hide the enjoyment he took from winding me up.

"Work of a true professional," I admitted.

"What is wrong with you two?" laughed Charlie, shaking her head. "After all that's happened, and you can notice the paintwork?"

"We've got the eye," said Young Dave knowingly.

"We sure do," I agreed, lacing my fingers behind my head, leaning back, and staring at the expert job. Suddenly, I jolted forward and told the others, "We need to check the garden. Just to be sure. Nothing rings true about this and if the police didn't find a murder weapon or some reason to explain how Sylvester died, then we need to. Who's with me?"

"You can count on me," said Young Dave, eagerly.

"If you think it will help," said Charlie, less than keen. "But you just checked."

"But three pairs of eyes are better than one. Come on. This whole situation stinks."

An hour later, we were none the wiser, just more sweaty and confused than ever. All we found were a few small pieces of wood splinters that could have come from the explosion or been there for any number of reasons.

We collapsed back onto the sofa in the living room and sat   there,   confounded   and   concerned.

Chapter 4

The living room door squeaked as it opened, making us jump. I needed a weapon handy just in case the murderer returned. Should I get one?

Charlie shrieked, Young Dave slapped his hands over his eyes—maybe believing it made him invisible—and even though my heart hammered in my chest, I readied to confront the assassin.

"Oh, it's Harlow," I blurted, smiling at Charlie who sighed then laughed.

Young Dave peeked from between his fingers, then relaxed and asked, "You named him Harlow? Cool."

Harlow raced into the room in that juddery way squirrels do, then sat and curled his tail around his body. He squeaked at us, cocked his head to the side, and waited.

"Is it just me, or is it like Harlow's talking to us?" I asked, feeling rather silly.

"I was just thinking the same thing," said Charlie, leaning forward to study him.

"Maybe he is. Maybe he's really smart and knows who the murderer is," mused Young Dave.

"He can't. He was falling from a tree, remember? And we don't know there was a murder. Maybe it was an accident." I sighed, getting the familiar scent of the fresh paint and underlying tone of Aunty Clem's pine floor cleaner, then leaned back on the sofa and watched Harlow as he scampered around in front of us, then lifted a tiny leg and held it up.

"Now he's pointing," said Charlie, edging forward further, grinning. "Maybe he is smart."

"Told you," said Young Dave smugly.

"He's probably just annoyed about his tree getting messed up and now he's afraid to go home. Is that it, Harlow? Are you worried about going home?"

Harlow nodded, I swear he did, making us gasp. He shook himself out from head to tail, causing a rainbow of dust to swirl around his red fur. He sneezed, which made him jump, so launched onto the arm of the sofa next to Young Dave and sat there, as if waiting for something.

"That squirrel keeps looking at me," stammered Young Dave with a nervous glance at the cute little guy.

"Young Dave, don't be a bloody fool," I groaned.

"Ha, that's a pound in the swear jar. Don't forget."

"Damn! Haven't had to pay all week, either."

Young Dave smiled smugly as he dashed off to get the jar, and I turned my attention back to the squirrel. "Were you vibing Young Dave?" I asked with a chuckle. "Do you want a snack? I guess you don't eat sandwiches, but let's see what I have in here, eh?" I dragged my tool bag over and opened it, my stomach growling. Harlow bounced around the sofa excitedly.

"Lucas Moran, how can you eat at a time like this?" said Charlie with a frown as I delved inside and shifted paintbrushes around.

"What? This craziness has made me ravenous. And I didn't get morning tea and cake, not even elevenses. Now it's past lunchtime. Are we still having bangers and mash for dinner?"

"Are you serious? What about Clem?"

"I think they feed them while they're in the hospital."

"I meant worrying about her. And visiting. Not to mention the mess here. And that poor man being killed. It's got to take priority."

"And it will. I mean, it does. But I think better on a full stomach. You want one?" I asked, offering the pack of Jaffa Cakes, which was no longer half full. Young Dave came back into the living room, jangling the swear jar as I studied the pack suspiciously. His eyes drifted to my hand then he turned to go back out. "Oi, have you been nicking my Jaffa Cakes again?"

"I just had the one! It was to calm my nerves."

"Hmm. May as well finish the pack then," I said, taking two then offering the pack to Young Dave who grabbed it eagerly.

"You two are impossible," tutted Charlie, but when Young Dave passed her the pack she took it shamelessly.

Harlow scrambled around the back of the sofa, so I searched through my emergency snacks and found a dusty bag of unsalted peanuts. As I opened them, he paused beside Charlie's head and sniffed. With a single leap, he landed on my lap and sat, eyes fixed on the nuts.

"Guess he really was hungry."

"He's had a stressful day too," said Charlie, wiping the sheen of sweat from her forehead, clearly worried Harlow was going to attack her or something.

"You okay?"

"I thought he might jump on my head, or bite us. They do that, you know?"

"I think that's territorial, but he seems friendly enough. Want to give him the nuts?"

Harlow and I turned to Charlie, and she giggled as she said, "I'm sorry, Harlow, I know you're a nice guy. It's just I got bitten by a mean grey squirrel when I was young. But I like you."

I passed her the nuts, so Harlow sprang onto her lap and sat patiently while Charlie tipped a palm of peanuts out. Harlow delved in immediately, taking one then sitting and eating it, getting crumbs all over Charlie, before taking the next. I munched on a sandwich while Young Dave pulled out a sausage roll from his overalls, and Charlie accepted a sandwich without too much persuasion.

We spent a quiet five minutes filling our bellies, then when the peanuts were gone Harlow hopped down and returned to his spot by the door, thumping his tail on the floor.

"He's definitely trying to tell us something," I noted.

"It's a squirrel," said Young Dave with a shrug. "What could he tell us?"

"I don't know, but this day couldn't get any more weird, so I'm going to play along. We need to do something. Although we do have to finish the decorating."

"Today? What if we get murdered?"

"Then the job will have to be put on hold," I laughed, slapping him on the back.

"I think we should follow him," said Charlie.

With embarrassed nods to each other, we nevertheless followed Harlow out into the hall. He ran over to the stairs again and sat on the bottom step, head cocked.

"Fine. What do you want us to do?" I asked.

He twitched his tail then bounded up the stairs.

"Stop him! Aunty will have a fit if that squirrel messes with her attic."

"Harlow," interrupted Charlie.

"Yes, thank you for that. If he gets into the attic and shreds whatever's left, Aunty will go apoplectic."

"Word of the day?" asked Charlie.

"Maybe," I mumbled. It was. I'd got the email first thing in the morning and had been waiting to use it ever since.

We chased after Harlow up the wide stairs, but he stopped suddenly on the half landing, causing Young Dave to try to jump over him, but his gangly limbs got caught in Charlie's legs and as they toppled I fell over the mess of bodies and landed on top of them both. Harlow climbed several steps and began to make a racket before jumping onto my back and bouncing up and down.

With a groan, I rolled over and helped untangle the others. Then we sat there, laughing as nervous tension was released.

"These stairs are a death trap." I rubbed at my elbow where I'd got a carpet burn. "Are you both okay?"

"I'm fine," said Charlie.

"Me too," grumbled Young Dave. "This is where Clem fell?"

"It's where she landed. She said she was halfway down then fell. Tripped, she said. I assume she missed a step and took a tumble. It's not like her, but everyone's slid off a tread and almost gone crashing down, right?"

"I've fallen down our stairs loads," admitted Young Dave.

"I never have," said Charlie proudly. "They really are lovely stairs, though. It's always been my favourite part of the house. The wood's in perfect condition, so dark and polished, and the red carpet runner and brass bars are so timeless."

"Aunty polishes the oak every week, and is very proud of the fact it's in better condition than when it was first installed."

We studied the staircase, rather an anomaly for the time as it was definitely more Georgian in style, built at a period when two styles were both in vogue, Georgian waning, Victorian ascending. The oak had darkened over the decades, and gleamed from the waxes and polishes Aunty had used every week for fifty years. The handrail was so smooth and perfect you could see your reflection, the curves as it took the turns so incredibly well crafted you couldn't find the join. The spindles were chunky and quite decorative, and the newel posts at the top, bottom, and the one beside us on the half landing were like works of art, the balls on top reminding me of shiny bald heads tanned in the sun.

"Oh no, what's that?" I gasped, pale wood catching my eye where Harlow sat on a step three up from the landing, head cocked, waiting patiently.

"What is it?" asked Charlie.

"The wood's damaged. Looks like a nick."

We crawled up closer and sure enough there was a small chunk out of the wood near to the tread in line with the riser. "That's weird, looks like a little hole, and there's a dent beside it. Like someone's hit it with a hammer."

"And look at this," gasped Young Dave from the left.

We rearranged ourselves so we could all see. Young Dave teased a piece of sturdy red string between his fingers, then held it taught. It was wrapped tight around a protruding nail in the side of the stairs, about ten centimetres long.

We stared at the string, then at each other, then at Harlow. I laughed, a nervous laugh, then said, "Harlow truly is a smart squirrel. I think we need to rename him Harlow Holmes."

"He's a real sleuth," said Charlie.

We watched the happy squirrel racing back and forth on the step, then my eyes were drawn back to the nail and string. I took the string in my fingers then traced an imaginary line from it across to the nick in the wood on the right-hand side.

"Is everyone thinking what I'm thinking?"

"That Clem's accident was no accident?" asked Charlie.

"That someone messed up her stairs by nailing string across to trip her up?" Young Dave shouted, causing Harlow to hop onto his shoulder and chatter in his ear. Young Dave freaked out, jumped up suddenly, and sped up the stairs as Harlow dropped onto the banister then slid halfway down before springing onto my shoulder.

I patted his tiny head and he calmed, then leaped onto the step and sat, ears twitching.

"Someone tried to murder Aunty Clem," I whispered, although I wasn't sure why. "Or at the very least tried to hurt her. Which they did. Those..."

"Don't forget the swear jar," Young Dave called down from the top step, looking sheepish after his undignified display.

"Those meanies," I sighed.

"Why would they do that? And what, they managed to get one nail out after cutting the string, but must have got interrupted?" asked Charlie.

"It's oak. Very old oak," I explained. "It gets as hard as iron over the years, so they probably tried and failed to pull it out." I knelt, then inspected the wood again. "Someone would have heard, surely?"

"You two make loads of noise," said Charlie. "Banging ladders and clattering your buckets. You said yourself, you put new nails into the woodwork, so someone could have timed it right then done the string any time. That wouldn't make a sound."

"Why am I suddenly getting a very bad feeling about this?" I asked, a knot forming in my stomach at the thought of someone purposely trying to cause an elderly lady to fall down her own stairs. It could kill her, or certainly incapacitate her.

"It had to be one of her group, right?" said Young Dave, sitting on the top step. "It must have been done once Clem was downstairs, and before she went back up again."

"Yes, but after she went up to get her Tarot. And they were in the dining room when she went up there. How is that even possible?"

"You're forgetting her form of exercise," said Charlie. "She always boasts about taking the stairs two at a time to keep her legs strong. So she would always miss the third step."

"Now that is some seriously good amateur sleuthing," I whistled, grinning at her.

"I have my moments."

"Every moment is perfect with you," I gushed.

"Ugh, guys, enough with the lovey dovey," groaned Young Dave.

"We can't help it. We haven't been married long," I said.

"So what? You were together for five years before that. I was only twelve then."

"Way to make us feel old," said Charlie, smiling at me.

"You're only as old as the woman you feel," I laughed, then turned serious when I realised just how dire the situation was. "Guys, what are we going to do? Someone tried to really hurt, if not kill, Aunty Clem, and who knows what else is booby-trapped around here? And I'm not liking the fact there are no police around. It just seems weird."

"Then call the DI and get them to come over. These are clues, and they shouldn't have missed them," said Charlie.

"You're right. Let's just check the attic first, see what the deal is, then I'll call. I hope Aunty's okay. Think I should check in?"

"She's in safe hands," said Charlie. "Let her rest. We'll visit later. And yes, you can have sausage and mash."

"Yes!" I glanced up at Young Dave, whose head was down, and nodded to Charlie to look. She caught his sudden change in mood and nodded back to me, then, as if it was her idea, said brightly, "Young Dave, would you like to join us for dinner? I've got loads of sausages that need eating today, so you'd be doing me a favour. Maybe we could visit Clem first, then you can come back to ours. I know it's your gym and pub night, but maybe you could skip that today?"

Young Dave brightened instantly, and said, "That would be great. Beats a Pot Noodle. Lucas, you okay with us missing the gym and a few pints?"

"Sure thing, buddy. Charlie's sausage and mash is famous. And that onion gravy, oh boy."

"You got a deal," he almost squealed, eyes shining, neck flushed with happiness.

Young Dave tried to spend as little time at home as possible, having a very awkward relationship with his parents. It wasn't that they were bad people, they were just not very well-suited to raising children. His dad worked away all week, returning on a Friday where he would set about trying to drain all available booze within a five-mile radius, focusing on the local Aldi as it had the cheapest cider. He was basically comatose until Monday morning when he'd crawl out of bed at an ungodly hour and be off driving a truck up and down the country until Friday when it would happen all over again, same as it had as long as Young Dave could remember.

His mum was the opposite. A teetotal terror of blame. Young Dave slept late until she left the house for work and tried to sneak back in after she was asleep. We tried to keep him at ours for dinner a few times a week so he got plenty of food, and it was why I went to the gym with him. Plus, I liked the daft lump of skin and bone. He would turn into a fine man in a few years. Ever since taking him on as an apprentice, I'd felt it my duty to look out for him and teach him what little I knew about the world that was worth passing on to eager ears and an inquisitive, if rather slow to get going, mind.

Bored with talk of sausages, Harlow zig-zagged up and down the stairs, chattering excitedly, seemingly now well and truly over his earlier shock.

"What should we do?" I asked Charlie. "I think we better let him lead the way. He seems to know a lot more about this than anyone else. How did he know about the string and nails?"

"Maybe he saw through the half landing window," mused Charlie. "Or maybe he's a magic squirrel and just senses it."

"He might be a sniffer squirrel," offered Young Dave. "You know, like a tracker. Sniffing out the bad guys."

"Is that what you are, Harlow?" I asked the now still squirrel. "Are you a magical tracking squirrel?"

"He just nodded!" shrieked Charlie. "Did you see that?"

"I did," I admitted. "Okay Harlow, lead the way."

Harlow leaped onto the banister, then scurried up to the top landing and the hall. We chased after him, finally about to see what remained of Aunty's attic of magical delights.

Chapter 5

Doors to the four bedrooms and bathroom led off the broad landing, and a narrow set of stairs hugged a wall as they switched back and up to the attic. The newel post and spindles were much plainer, but the handrail was still a work of art and everything was in as good a condition as the main stairs. Reserved for servants' quarters when first built, Aunty had slowly but surely begun to use the top of the house for various hobbies over the years, finally settling into her ever-increasing collection of all things paranormal. I hadn't been up here for at least a year, as Aunty liked to have a private room where she could, in her own words, "Really be herself and let her hair down."

The door was open, so we filed in and tried not to look out of the large gap where the window had been. Ragged edges of brick and the exposed lintel above the opening afforded a great view of the houses across the road and their expansive gardens, but it was very high and very dangerous. I had no idea if the floor had been compromised, but it seemed solid enough, so I decided to risk it. I went in first, mindful of Aunty's artefacts and who knew what else that littered the bare floorboards.

The roof actually didn't seem as bad as I'd imagined, but it would take a professional to repair it. A long bench that Aunty worked at under the window was missing a leg so had toppled over, spilling jars, vials, books, a rack of chemicals, along with bunches of herbs, more pestles and mortars than anyone could possibly need, and things I simply couldn't fathom at all.

"At least her books are mostly still intact," said Charlie, running a finger along the wide bookcase brimming with numerous leather-bound books.

"What is all this stuff?" asked Young Dave, picking up a jar of what looked like pickled pig trotters. "Is that a human skull? Cool." He grabbed the skull from a shelf on the opposite wall and wiggled the jaw.

"I can't believe there isn't more damage. It's like it was designed to just blow out the window," said Charlie.

"She does most of her potion making and reading at the bench, so if she messed up and something happened, I guess it would mostly take out the window. But yeah, it's still weird." I noted the numerous crystal balls and packs of Tarot still neatly aligned on the shelves on the side wall, along with several prized books, and a stick about a foot long that caught my attention for some reason.

I wandered over and picked up the length of wood no thicker than my finger. My hand tingled and I almost dropped it in shock. The pale wood was smooth and warm and slightly misshapen. A cool twig is what you'd think if you saw it, but I had a sneaking suspicion this was no ordinary stick.

"I think this is her wand," I said, swishing it back and forth. The wood grew warmer in my hand, and for the briefest of moments I was sure it fizzed at the end, like a dying sparkler on Bonfire Night, when you'd immediately pester your mum for another one. "Whoa! Did you see that?"

Charlie turned, holding her own nice stick, and asked, "See what? And I think this must be her wand. It was under the bench. It has her initials carved into it at the thicker end." Charlie sidestepped the mess and held it up to show me.

"Is it warm? This one is."

Charlie frowned. "Not really. Just feels like a lovely stick. It is very smooth, and I like the slight bend to it. I still can't believe she actually has a wand."

"That is so cool," gushed Young Dave, replacing the skull and joining us.

"Maybe this one's a spare," I shrugged, then adjusted my grip so I could check for a name. I read it with surprise. "Lucas. It's got my name on it. Was she going to give me a wand?"

"Looks like it," chuckled Charlie. "Maybe you can be a wizard and join her coven."

"Don't make jokes. She hates it. She takes this stuff seriously, you know. They all do. They were up at the crack of dawn doing unspeakable things in the woods this morning."

"Dancing around naked and summoning fairies," laughed Young Dave.

"Maybe not fairies. She's always said it's for gathering energy into the coven, calling on benevolent spirits to give them power, that kind thing."

"And now you have a wand of your very own," chided Charlie. But then she turned serious and asked, "Do you think there's anything to it? The magic, I mean?"

"Honestly, I don't think so. Maybe there are energies around us, forces we can't see, but magic? Although..." I was about to mention how the wand sparkled and was warm, but decided I was being silly. Just a trick of the light pouring through the hole and reflecting off the shattered glass and the crystal balls.

"Yes?" asked Charlie.

"Nothing, just being silly. Now, where's Harlow? We need to get him to help us."

We hunted the room, a large space that took up the entire footprint of the house apart from where it had been boarded out for storage space under the eaves. Aunty Clem had gone to town with her new hobby. Everything from crystals to dreamcatchers, to bizarre objects made of brass with more cogs than could possibly be functional, she had an astonishing array of objects. Clearly, most hadn't been touched in a long time, and merely stored away from the main space by the window.

What she focused on, and was evident from what she had told me over the years and especially recently, were spells and potions.

"That reminds me," I called out.

"What does? You haven't said anything else," said Charlie with a smile, knowing how I got sometimes.

"Sorry, I was just thinking about Aunty's stuff. Where's her spellbook? She wanted us to find it, remember? She was worried someone might steal it. Maybe they tried, and blew up the place on purpose."

"My guess is at her work bench," said Charlie, so we weaved our way back over to the toppled bench. We sifted through the glass carefully, mindful of the chemicals and herbs just in case we caused a chain reaction, and the longer we searched the more I felt that this was silly and dangerous and we shouldn't be here.

"Let's call it quits," I said. "This place literally blew up. Twice. It's too risky. What if something happens to one of you?"

"Or to you," said Charlie.

"I'm more worried about you guys. Young Dave, let's leave."

"It's gotta be here, I'm sure."

"Why are you so interested?" I asked.

"Because Clem wanted it, right? It's important to her. She'll be gutted if it's lost. Think maybe a firefighter stole it?" His eyes widened.

"What would a firefighter want with a book full of pretend spells?" I asked.

"Dunno. Maybe they thought they could sell it?"

"No, come on, let's go." I stood, then jumped a mile when Harlow dropped from the exposed beams and landed on a plain wooden box beside the fallen bench. He sprang up and down, chattering, then actually stamped a leg.

"Are you thinking what I'm thinking??" I asked the others.

"That three sausages would be amazing for dinner?" said Young Dave.

"That Harlow likes boxes?" said Charlie with a frown.

"Or," I suggested with a sigh, "that the book is in the box. Is it, Harlow? And yes, three sausages would be optimal."

"Optimal? You don't get optimal sausages," said Charlie.

"You do," said Young Dave, nodding sagely along with me.

"Harlow, do you want to show us?" I asked.

Harlow grunted, then launched from the box onto my shoulder and wrapped his tail around my neck. I bent and retrieved the box, then stood and opened it.

"Oh boy."

Charlie and Young Dave crowded round, eager to see what I'd discovered. With my two shadows, I moved over to a bench jammed against the wall and put down the box. Inside were several notebooks thick with pages, tied with string. Beneath, taking up almost the entire space, was a robust leather-bound book. Carved inexpertly into the cover were the words, *Clem's Book of Spells*. I hefted the weighty tome and flipped it over. The back was blank, so I placed it down and looked at the others. "Think I should open it?"

"Course you should," said Young Dave, eyes glued to the book.

"I don't know. It's kind of private," said Charlie.

"Yeah, you're right. It is. There could be anything in there."

"Like what?" asked Young Dave, reaching out for the book.

I slapped his hand away and said, "I don't know. Private thoughts. Pictures of naked old men in Speedos."

"Gross." Young Dave scrunched up his face and moved his hand away.

"Let's leave it on the shelf so we know it's safe, then I'm calling that DI and they can come and do a bloody proper job."

"Forfeit!" shouted Young Dave with glee.

"Fine, I'll put it in the swear jar later. Come on, let's get downstairs and put the kettle on. I'm parched. Haven't had a proper cuppa since first thing this morning."

Harlow bounced along in front, seemingly happy we'd done a good job, then disappeared somewhere. Maybe to have a nap.

I went out into the garden to call the DI again. He answered almost immediately and I told him I had some news but he needed to come in person. He promised to be right over, which, again, was weird, so I hung up. Since when were the police so fast to react? Over the last few years, all emergency services had been so stretched that ambulance waiting times could often be hours, the NHS was overflowing with full beds, fire brigades couldn't cope, and the police were beyond harried. But for us, they'd been and gone within hours, and DIs, who should be busy, come immediately when you call and answer on the first ring.

Then I slapped my head and went back inside to tell the others what I'd just realised. How could I have forgotten?

"She's getting special treatment," I blurted, causing Charlie to pause halfway through pouring boiling water into three mugs.

"Who is?"

"Aunty Clem. I mean, since when do you get taken to the hospital for a broken arm and immediately get given a bed and have doctors and nurses checking on you like that? They haven't got the room. It normally takes hours."

"She's old, and was badly hurt," said Young Dave, eyeing the tea warily as he liked his teabag removed before it got too strong.

"And there could have been a head injury," said Charlie as she finished pouring, then slapped Young Dave's hand away as he tried to retrieve his teabag. She fished it out with a spoon, then added two sugars to mine and Young Dave's before treating herself with a half spoonful.

"Yes, I know all that, but it's still unusual. And what about here? Forensics have been, there's no police tape, and the DI's got to work immediately. And there are no police anywhere in sight. It's not how it's meant to happen. The place should be sealed off. Sylvester had a hole right through him. Well, almost, but you know what I mean. That's serious. It might be snipers or terrorists, or anything."

"What are you going on about, Lucas? Maybe they aren't busy and leaped at something to do," said Charlie, handing me my tea.

"Thanks. No, I'm right about this. It's because of Uncle Bill. Remember, his name was funny because he was high up in the Old Bill."

"What's Old Bill?" asked Young Dave.

We turned to him and asked, "Seriously?"

"Must be a generation thing," he shrugged, then slurped his tea and smiled. "Lovely cuppa."

"They still say Old Bill to mean police, don't they?" I asked Charlie.

"I thought they did."

"Nope, they call them cops now. Anyway, whatever. What's the point? My tea needs a biscuit, and it won't dunk itself. I want to put my feet up. All this investigating is exhausting."

I rolled my eyes, then continued. "Uncle Bill was a high-ranking constable or something like that. A bit before my time as he was retired when I was young, but he was well-respected and knew everyone. Aunty still gets visits from the old-timers who they used to know back in the day. She was loved by everyone, and they used to throw parties for all the cops and Uncle Bill hosted barbecues, that kind of thing. I bet some of his old cronies heard what happened, or the younger ones knew of him, and made sure to try to get this sorted without any fuss so Aunty can be safe and come home without being confronted with crime scene tape. Last thing she'd want was for this to hit the news."

The doorbell rang so I went to answer it, not as surprised as I should have been to find DI Durham scowling when I peered through the peephole.

"This better be good," he growled as I opened the door and he barged in without waiting to be invited.

"Lovely to see you too," I said, smiling, as I knew it would annoy him.

"Can we please get to the point? I'm a busy man."

"But not too busy to come over here straight away when I called, or to arrive the moment you heard about the murder this morning."

"And your point is?"

"Look, I don't know why you're being so rude, but this is important. We're freaked out here. There's no crime scene tape, no police presence, and it's like the whole thing never happened. Isn't anyone concerned we'll get blown up?"

"Hello," said Charlie, attempting to halt my tirade.

"Charlie, DI Durham. DI Durham, this is Charlie, my wife. You've met Young Dave already."

"I sure have," he sighed, rubbing at his three-day stubble then running his hands through his thinning brown hair. His eyes were dark, and deeply sunk, and you could just tell he was a boozer. Un-ironed shirt, faded black trousers, and cheap shoes meant he most likely lived alone.

"Hi again," said Young Dave, rigid by the stairs.

"Never met someone who introduces themselves as Young Dave before," DI Durham grumbled.

"That's his name," I said, frowning.

"Is it? He was named Young Dave?"

"Well, no, obviously. But it saves any confusion."

"Because you know so many Daves?"

"Doesn't everyone?" I looked to Young Dave and Charlie for support, and they both nodded eagerly.

"I know quite a few," said Charlie.

"My Dad's called Dave," said Young Dave. "Imagine how confusing it would be if I just had the same name."

"Your parents could have called you something else." DI Durham scowled as his eyes took in the entrance hall then shifted over to the stairs, like he was searching for something.

"You need to explain things to us. It feels wrong," I said.

"Fine, what do you want to know?" asked DI Durham.

"How come it was so speedy? It's not normal, is it?"

"No, it really isn't. May I sit? And do I smell tea?"

"I'll make you a cup," offered Charlie. After she got his milk and sugar preferences, she went to get his tea. Young Dave and I took ours into the living room and sat on chairs, leaving him the sofa.

"Nice ceiling. And the skirting boards look like they were just installed. You busy next week?"

"Always busy. But we can do you in a month if it's a quick job."

"The whole house needs redecorating. I don't have the time, the inclination, the skill, or the equipment. Let me know when you're available."

"I'll email you," said Young Dave brightly. "I've got the address on your card, and I can check the spreadsheet later."

"Spreadsheet? Bit different to how it used to be, eh?"

"Tell me about it," I chuckled. "Young Dave wanted us to build an app."

"Would have been easy," he grumbled.

Charlie came in with her and DI Durham's tea and sat at the other end of the sofa.

"So, as you might have noticed, things moved rather quickly here. Your aunty was apparently married to some bigwig and everyone liked him. There are still those on the force who remember him well and the moment they heard about this the word came down through the various channels that it was to be dealt with quickly, efficiently, and discreetly."

"I knew it!"

"But it's less than ideal. Normally, I'd take a good day to cover a scene with my partner, and we'd have at least a dozen constables checking on everything. We had a morning. But we got what we needed, and the boss is happy. Meaning, I won't get a rollicking. Anything else?"

"Yes, who do you think did it? And how?"

"And why?" said Charlie.

"Ah, I understand now. You think it was one of her, what did she call it? Her coven? All into magic, apparently. Bunch of kooks. Apart from your aunt, of course. You're thinking it had to be one of them. It happened while they were in the garden after the explosion. We still have them in for questioning, you'll be pleased to know, which is why I got here so fast. It's a short drive, but I need to get back to it. That Mike character is a handful, and Shirley is fretting about her dinner. And as for Em, well, she seems like a sweet girl caught up in something she doesn't understand. What's with this magic stuff?"

"Just a hobby of Aunty Clem's. It keeps her out of trouble."

"You might want to rephrase that. Look, they insist it's for real. That magic and spells and whatnot are real. I have an open mind, and each to their own, but it's got a ring of darkness to it."

"Black magic, you mean?" I asked.

"Maybe," he shrugged. He sipped his tea, deep in thought, then clearly came to a decision. "Okay, cards on the table here?"

"Sure."

"I think your aunt was messing with chemicals she didn't understand, blew out the attic by accident, then tripped on the stairs. My guess is that something came flying over the house and went right through Sylvester. Problem being, we can't find it. But it's a logical explanation. Some large round object shot over the house and killed him. We searched thoroughly, but there was nothing. If you don't mind, I'd like to bring a team back here later on and see if we discover anything. That okay?"

"Of course."

"But keep it to yourselves. The bosses want this kept hush hush and nobody is meant to know, so we put the attic down as a gas explosion to save your aunt any embarrassment. This sounding good so far?"

"Yes, brilliant. We looked in the garden, too, and found nothing. Can something do that?"

"I looked into you, Lucas. You're an army guy, so you know the same as I do that when anything travels fast enough it can kill. Even tear right through a person. My money is on that having happened. Clem blew up her own attic by accident and something sailed over the wrong way, one of those freak accidents, and did for Sylvester the accountant. There's no murder suspect, but we have to question everyone anyway. Go by the book. Relax, it's all over. The attic is safe, and there is no mysterious assassin."

"That does make sense," said Charlie.

"But everything flew out the front," said Young Dave.

"Like I said, a freak occurrence. If it sailed up high enough or maybe bounced off that tree out front, it could have got into the back garden. We'll look again later."

"That sounds plausible, I guess, but we have to show you something."

"As long as it's the door, or another cup of tea, I'm a happy man."

He drained his tea so Charlie instantly said, "I'll make you another."

DI Durham grunted his thanks, so we led him out into the entrance hall and waited in awkward silence until Charlie returned. The man must have had a tongue impervious to heat as he gulped half his tea then wiped his mouth on his shirt sleeve. "That was good. It's thirsty work conducting interviews. Even when they don't stop talking." He gave Young Dave the daggers, who, for once, decided the best thing was to remain silent.

Chapter 6

Keen to get involved, Young Dave showed the DI the remains of the trip wire, or trip string, as we gathered around awkwardly on the stairs. He frowned as Young Dave explained, clearly not very impressed with our levels of detective work, then bent to inspect the nail hole and the remaining nail and string once the admittedly rather long-winded explanation was done.

DI Durham stood with a grunt then put his hands on his hips and leaned back a little to straighten out with an audible click.

"Damn back is giving me so much trouble lately."

We stared at him, waiting, but he just got a faraway look in his eyes and began to mumble.

"You okay?" I asked.

"Yes, fine, just thinking. It's what us detectives do. We think. Which is why," he cast an accusing glance at us in turn, "we're professionals. Look, I'm sure you think there's a big conspiracy and someone's out to get your aunt, but you have to consider the alternative."

"That there's more than one of them?" gasped Charlie.

"No, that nobody is out to get Clem. That her attic issues are the result of her rather strange hobby and she tripped after the explosion."

"I already told you," I said, losing my patience. "The attic exploded after she tripped. I was here. I heard it."

"Yes, but maybe there was a smaller one first, and it set off the main one. And there was one after that."

"So what about the string and nails? How do you explain that then?" asked Young Dave, looking miffed.

"Could have been here for years," he shrugged. "It's most likely a guide the carpenters used to line up the runner, or something like that. You see it all the time in old houses. Remains of things that have gone unnoticed for years."

"Not in this house, and certainly not on these stairs. Aunty Clem goes over them once a week with her polish and wax and that's why they're in such great condition. She'd have noticed. And besides, the nail would catch on the Hoover. She's always vacuuming."

"Even at her age?" asked DI Durham, looking doubtful.

"Yes, even at her age," I said, scowling. "She's in her seventies."

"Yeah, she's not a centurion," said Young Dave.

"I think you mean centenarian," I corrected.

"Why would someone want to trip her up? Why would anyone risk getting caught banging nails into the wood then having to try to remove them?" he asked.

"I thought you said that was your job?" I snapped.

"No need to get defensive. I'm just trying to look for an explanation. Usually, the obvious one is the right one. And I'm seeing a nail and some string. You said you were here right after she fell and everyone else was downstairs. After her fall, did you leave her alone?"

"No, I don't think so. Oh, that's right, Mike watched her after I'd gone outside, and when Young Dave arrived he was here for a while, but I don't think anyone else was."

We stared at Young Dave, who reddened under the scrutiny and blurted, "It wasn't me! I didn't try to murder Clem."

"Of course not, son," soothed DI Durham.

"What about Mike?" asked Charlie.

"He watched Clem, but that was after Sylvester got killed," I said.

"So how could someone have come and removed the nail?" asked DI Durham. "It's doubtful Mike had a hammer on him, and besides, Clem would have seen, so if there was another nail, how did it come out?"

"Maybe it wasn't in tight enough, and it fell out. This wood is very hard," I suggested.

"Or, this short piece of string has been here for who knows how long, and Clem simply tripped. But don't worry, we have everyone who was here still at the station, and we will get to the bottom of this. Rest assured, my top priority is to ensure we discover who killed Sylvester, if he was, in fact, killed. Which, he wasn't."

"He looked dead to me," I snapped.

DI Durham stared at me in confusion, then said, "You know what I mean. That someone did it on purpose."

"So you're saying someone did?"

"No, absolutely not."

We trailed after the detective down into the hall where he drained his tea, handed the mug to Charlie, and said, "Thank you for the tea. I'll be in touch the moment there's a breakthrough, and in the meantime try not to get too many ideas into your heads. These things usually play out pretty fast, and just to be on the safe side, I'll send a team back over in a few hours to go over everything once again. But remember, this is on the quiet, as my boss is on my back to get this wrapped up and he downright ordered me to ensure this stayed quiet and didn't cause any problems for Clem."

"I think a guy being killed in your garden is already a problem, and someone trying to make you fall down the stairs."

"Yes, well, let's just keep a level head and see what the day brings, shall we?" With a nod, the DI let himself out and closed the door behind him.

"I don't like that guy," said Young Dave with a pout.

"Neither do I," agreed Charlie.

"He's definitely got a brusque manner. I don't buy his explanation about the stairs. It makes no sense. And the garden's been searched by the police, and us, and there's nothing there that could have killed Sylvester, so it's obvious someone killed him."

"But how?" said Charlie.

"I have no idea," I admitted, feeling beaten down by the day.

Harlow came racing in from the kitchen, then skidded on the gleaming tiles, crashing into Young Dave's leg. He turned to me and began chattering away excitedly, then rushed back into the kitchen, returned when he realised no one was following him, and began gesticulating wildly.

"What is with that squirrel?" I asked, scratching my head and wondering if I could take a quick nap.

"He's like Lassie," said Young Dave seriously. "He's trying to tell us something. He wants us to follow him."

"Yes, thank you, Young Dave for stating the blindingly obvious. What I meant was, how is he so smart? Squirrels hide nuts and do daft things in trees, they don't go around murder scenes pointing out the clues for you. It's uncanny."

"Maybe his fall did something to his brain," said Charlie. "It happens to people. They get a bump on the head and suddenly they can speak French."

"If he starts saying 'Je m'appelle Harlow,' then I'll believe it," I grumbled.

"Stop being such a grump," said Charlie softly, and put her hand to my shoulder. "Are you okay?" she asked, looking deep into my eyes.

"Yeah, just tired and stressed. I hope Aunty's okay."

"She'll be fine. We just have to hold it together for her sake and make sure she gets better as soon as possible."

"I know, you're right. But this stuff she's involved in, strangers in the house every week. I don't like it. They could be up to anything."

"It's just a hobby," said Charlie. "Some company for her." Charlie checked around us, then got closer to me and Young Dave and whispered, "And besides, I'm beginning to think this isn't just a hobby. I think she really does know a few things about magic."

"Very funny," I chuckled. "You had me going for a minute there."

"Lucas, I'm serious. Wasn't your mum into magic too? You said she used to be. When they were both very young. They're sisters, so maybe it runs in the family."

"She did, but only when she was a kid. They're both very secretive about it. Mum dismisses it as foolish nonsense."

"There you go then. Maybe there's something to it."

"But I've never seen Mum actually do any magic, and I haven't seen Clem do any either."

"Maybe they're sworn to secrecy," suggested Young Dave.

"It's not very secret if you hold a coven in your house every Friday evening, apart from the odd day when you get up early and go prancing about in the woods," I said.

"I meant, maybe they can't actually show you stuff. Maybe it's against the rules or something. That you have to be a part of the club. Er, the coven, I mean."

Harlow began going apoplectic—word of the day again!—from the kitchen doorway, so I sighed and said, "Let's go see what Lassie wants," and with a weak smile of sympathy from Charlie, she took my hand and we followed Young Dave as he skipped after Harlow, seemingly very pleased to be having a day of intrigue and mystery rather than giving the living room walls and woodwork the once over.

With a longing look at the seasoned Le Crueset frying pan in the kitchen—Aunty Clem made the best bacon and egg sandwiches this side of Cardiff—I dutifully trudged after the others, keen to put this mad day behind me and stare at a white wall until my eyes went funny.

The familiar, stunning scents of Aunty's garden hit with full force under the afternoon sun. It brought back memories of coming here after school and on the weekends when I was young, Aunty and Mum sitting in the garden gossiping while I chased after bees, made dens in the small wild woodland area at the end of the garden, or looked for frogs around the pond. I always adored catching tadpoles with a little fishing net and putting them in a jar to go and show before returning them to the water. It felt like a lifetime ago now, especially with Mum having been abroad for so long, but I'd always made it a point to visit Aunty Clem at least once a week even without Mum, even if it meant Dad sometimes having to struggle through the gossip about the town and the neighbours—a chatterbox he was not.

Harlow ran circles around us, bombarding us with a cascade of screeches, barks, and snorts.

"What's got into him?" I wondered.

"He's picked up on something, for sure," said Charlie.

"I told you, he's just like Lassie," said Young Dave with glee, bounding after Harlow as the red blur of fur raced halfway down the garden to where Sylvester had met his untimely and grisly demise, then darted into the herbaceous border on the right.

We caught up with them and all stood on the edge of the lawn where Harlow had gone into the undergrowth, and I said, "We already looked in there. I did, then you both did too. We searched everywhere and there's nothing there. What's that daft squirrel up to?"

Harlow launched from the greenery, bounced off a hydrangea, then landed on my shoulder and squealed in my ear before jumping onto Charlie's shoulder and doing the same.

"I'm guessing he really wants us to look again," she laughed.

Already sweating, and cursing how late in the day it was for getting the living room done, and a little confounded by why I had it fixed in my head that it had to be done today at all, I nevertheless carefully stepped into the border and eased aside the plants to check. Harlow landed beside me in the rich soil then disappeared under a hibiscus, the purple flowers dropping as he disturbed the delicate bush.

I pushed against the woody stems and gasped, then bent as low as I was able and reached out, before snatching my hand back and carefully retracing my steps, mindful of my foot placement.

"What is it?" asked Charlie, frowning in concern. "You look like you've seen a ghost."

"You are very pale, mate," said Young Dave, glancing around the garden nervously as if we were about to be attacked.

"Um, there's something there," I gasped, shaking my head, not quite able to process it.

"What?" asked Charlie, walking towards the plants.

"No, don't!" I shouted, reaching out to grab her arm.

"Lucas, what's wrong? What's in there?"

"It's... it's a crystal ball."

"It can't be. We checked there. We checked everywhere."

"I guess we didn't look hard enough," I sighed, wiping at my forehead.

"You mean the DI might be right?" asked Young Dave, eyes downcast.

"I think he might be," I admitted, although it just didn't ring true, not even now. "But we all searched, I know we did. It's got blood on it," I added.

"Let me see," said Charlie, smiling softly at me.

"Just be careful, and don't touch it. Damn, now I'll have to call the DI again. He's going to love this."

Charlie eased into the border, putting a single step into the soil then leaning forward and parting the plants. She gasped, then hopped back out with Harlow running around her feet and almost tripping her over.

"Careful!" I warned him, then scooped him up and let him sit on my shoulder. Since when did I have a pet squirrel? This day was getting beyond weird.

"You're right. It's a crystal ball. A bloody crystal ball!"

"Swear jar!" sang Young Dave.

"No, you muppet, she meant coated with blood."

"Um, yes, that's right," said a guilty looking Charlie. "I meant bloody as in blood." I winked at her and she smiled knowingly.

With a sigh, I braced myself then called the DI. He answered gruffly, then I told him what we'd found. He said he'd get the team over immediately, just to be done with it.

We milled about for twenty minutes, not quite knowing what to do with ourselves, then I met the DI and the team of three and led them around the side garden into the back. They cautiously retrieved the crystal ball then performed a very thorough search of everything under the watchful gaze of DI Durham.

An hour later, and with the search seemingly complete, the others left, having found nothing else, not even a footprint in the border. Not surprising, as even with Aunty Clem keen on mulching, the ground was dry and the plants were struggling because of the hosepipe ban.

"I think we can all agree that we have most likely found what killed Sylvester," said the DI, trying not to look smug and failing miserably.

"And that your team failed to find it earlier and it was us that did your job for you," I said curtly, in no mood for his attitude.

"Yes, well, as I said, we were going to return this afternoon."

"You guys rushed through your jobs because you wanted this hushed up, and because you didn't want to get told off by your bosses. That's utterly unprofessional and you should be ashamed of yourselves," said Charlie, staring him down until he lowered his eyes.

"It was an oversight. Nothing more."

"An oversight? A man died, and how long would you have kept those poor people at the station? Poor Shirley is getting on, and that young girl, Em, will probably be terrified. You failed to find the obvious, and if I hadn't spotted it how long would this have lasted, eh?"

"I'm sure we would have worked it out. After all, it was a very nasty injury. No weapon could cause a wound like that."

"That's not true. I've seen injuries like that, and numerous others," I said, pushing down the mental imagery. "But that's beside the point. You didn't seal off the area, evidence might be contaminated, and this could have gone on for days, weeks, or months without anyone knowing what happened, and Aunty's friends would have remained under suspicion. That's lax, bordering on incompetent."

"Now just one minute. You can't go accusing me of being incompetent. And I already told you it was obvious this was a terrible accident."

"You have people being interviewed under suspicion of murder because you and your team failed miserably at your jobs," snapped Charlie. "I think it's time you left."

DI Durham met my eye, and his features softened. "I truly am sorry. You're right, this should have been handled differently. I apologise. But I assure you, we didn't rush the search out here, and we did our jobs properly, but it wasn't the conventional way we do things. It's politics, and I hate it. Always have. But we all answer to somebody. But look, and I'm being honest here, I spoke to the team and they swear that each of them searched the garden, every single part of it, and looked where you found the crystal ball. They gave me their word they left no stone unturned." He shrugged.

"We checked too," said Young Dave. "I guess it's easy to overlook. Just a glass ball. It blends in, right?"

"It does," said the DI, "but that's no excuse. Maybe they're having an off day, or stressed over being bossed about and told to get this done asap, but still..."

"Yeah, well, sorry for shouting," I said. "It's been a bad day, and I'm worried about my aunt, but I guess that's it, case closed."

"We'll get the blood on the crystal ball checked within the hour, just to be sure, and I'll let you know, but I'm guessing it will match Sylvester's. So then, yes, that will be it, case closed. Sorry once again. I'll be in touch later."

We watched him leave, then Young Dave turned to us both and asked, "Are you thinking what I'm thinking?" with a wry smile.

I nodded. "If what you're thinking is that there is no way that team missed it the first time, and no way that we did either, then yes, that's exactly what I'm thinking."

Young Dave deflated, and admitted, "I was thinking it meant we could have an early dinner then go visit Clem."

"Muppet," I sighed.

"You're serious?" asked Charlie.

"Yes, I mean, come on. A bloody crystal ball sailed out the front of the house and what, hit a tree like the DI suggested earlier, then bounced over the roof and shot right through poor Sylvester? What are the chances of that happening and then at least six people looking in the spot it landed and nobody finding it? Bit far-fetched."

"But so is the idea that somebody killed Sylvester some other way, then snuck back in here and planted the crystal ball.

When did they do it? How come we didn't see or hear them? And how did they get blood on the crystal ball?"

"Guess we'll just have to find out ourselves, because I'll bet my best brushes that it's Sylvester's blood on it and the police will close this case faster than Young Dave saying yes to the offer of a fourth sausage."

"I can have four?" he gasped, practically salivating.

"Let's just have a cuppa." I would have preferred something stronger, but knew I'd be down the rabbit hole if I started drinking on a day like this when it was far from over.

As if to prove my point, Harlow caught our attention by talking loudly as usual, then raced down the garden and paused halfway before glancing back at us. Then he continued to the end where the small woodland area began.

"What   now?"   I   groaned.

Chapter 7

We made our way through the garden, but Charlie pulled me aside as Young Dave sped off ahead. "You mean it, don't you?"

"Am I being daft? It just doesn't ring true. It's very convenient, isn't it?"

"Unless we did miss the crystal ball and that is what happened."

"But do you believe that?"

"No." Charlie deflated and admitted, "I think someone's playing us, and the pieces are falling into place too easily. That detective is itching to put this behind him. I get where he's coming from, that he's being ordered about by his boss, but it simply doesn't feel right."

"Exactly! Too easy. Too obvious. Although, you know, not very obvious as whoever heard of something like this happening? No, there's more to this, and somebody planted that crystal ball the moment they had the chance. But it must have been recently, most likely after we checked the garden. But why wait? It would have been better if we'd found it earlier, surely?"

"Unless they couldn't get here before now?"

"Could be. Look, I know this isn't exactly the day off work you had in mind, but thanks for sticking around."

"Clem's family, and I like her, and if somebody is screwing with us then I want to help find out why. And Clem's distraught about Sylvester. We owe it to her, and him and his family, to find out what went on. Oh, his poor family. I hadn't even thought about them."

"He lived alone I think, but sure, he must have parents or brothers and sisters, but I suppose the police take care of all that. Think we should pay them a visit, offer our condolences?"

"We could do. Is that the done thing? We're strangers."

"Honestly, I don't know anything anymore. What a day. But are you with me on this, or am I being crazy and looking for answers when we should just take this for what it seems? An old lady was messing with her chemistry set and tripped down the stairs and it caused Sylvester's death?"

"No, I'm with you. There is definitely something going on here and it looks like it's down to us to figure it out."

"Then let's do exactly that."

We caught up with Young Dave and a very excitable Harlow right where the manicured garden gave way to a wildlife haven Aunty had been cultivating, or not cultivating, for decades. It wasn't very deep, then met a meandering stream with a little bridge before more trees led to open farmland, the fading scent of oil seed rape thick in the air even from here.

"What's he found now?" I asked Young Dave.

"Not sure. I was waiting for you guys, but he's very excited."

We watched Harlow bounding around, chattering away, then he rushed into the trees, clearly expecting us to follow.

"You'd think he would live down here, instead of out the front," said Charlie.

"I think he likes watching Aunty Clem come and go. Or maybe this is the grey squirrel's patch. Probably is, as I've seen plenty nipping out onto the lawn. Aunty always complains they dig it up to bury hazelnuts. Let's go see what he has in store for us this time. If it's a grenade, I'm going to bed."

We stepped into the welcome shade, the temperature several degrees cooler thanks to the thick canopy overhead. Harlow raced up a tree, swung from a branch, landed on another trunk, then ran down headfirst and sat there, waiting, ears twitching.

"They didn't check here, did they?" I said.

"Guess they figured it was too far from the scene. You have to stop searching somewhere," said Charlie with a shrug. "But I don't know. Maybe they did."

"Still doesn't seem right," I grumbled.

We stood around Harlow, waiting, but seemingly this was it, and he was going nowhere. I eased forward, not wanting to spook him, but he was unafraid. As I bent, he scrambled up the tree until he was level with my head and our eyes met. It was a strange sensation, almost like looking into a human's eyes. Those dark, beady orbs were full of intelligence, and if he'd begun to speak I wouldn't have been surprised.

"What have you found, Harlow?" I asked, inspecting the ground but finding nothing.

He made a strange *tsk* sound, like he was disappointed, then Charlie stepped forward, squatted beside me, and gasped. "I think he means this," she said, reaching out and easing out a length of red string snagged on a branch.

We stood, Charlie still holding the string which was caught at hand height, and we simply stared at it.

"What does this mean?" asked Young Dave.

"It means DI Durham's theory about the string being old is hogwash," I said. "No way that's been here for years and still looking like it came off a ball of string today. It's bright, clean, and new. It would be covered in moss and lichen, or at least dirty if it wasn't fresh. The woods are damp and this would be like everything else in here."

We took a moment to study the tiny woodland. Moss was soft underfoot and creeping up the trunks of the trees, everything was covered in lichen and lungwort, interspersed with weeds and struggling grasses. But mostly it was moss, apart from in the spring when daffodils lifted their sunny heads to declare warm weather was on the way, followed by bluebells and crocus, and small yellow flowers I didn't know the name of but always felt happy when they arrived.

"Another clue," gasped Young Dave, eyes wide.

"Looks that way," I said.

"But what does it mean?" he asked.

"It means that whoever booby-trapped Aunty came this way and the string caught on the tree. Or this is the part missing from her stairs and they lost it in a rush to get away. Charlie, what do you think?"

"I think you're right. There's no way any of this is an accident or coincidence. We need to call the DI back."

"And say what? We found some string? You know what he's like. He'll say it could have been here for years and that'll be the end of it. He's probably already filling out the paperwork before he gets his big red stamp and marks this case closed, a non-starter. No, this is down to us."

"We're going to solve a murder?" asked Young Dave dubiously. "That's nuts, mate. We might mess it up. Or get killed."

"Nobody's getting killed on my watch," I growled. "But there's no choice. According to Durham, this is already wrapped up. I bet the others are already being released and that'll be that."

Right on cue, my phone rang, so I answered, listened to what the caller had to say, then said, "Thanks for letting me know," before hanging up.

"Guess who?" I said.

"Durham?" Charlie smiled knowingly, understanding how stressed I was getting.

"Right. He said the blood matched, and again, that's swift police work. I thought doing that kind of thing took days. Oh, and one other thing, he said the others have been released, and are free to go about their business. Guess that's the end of it as far as he's concerned."

"When were they released, though?" asked Charlie. "And how did one of them come back and plant the crystal ball if they were at the police station?"

"That's just it, they weren't just released. He said it was, er, very annoying, although he used stronger language, but they were released almost as soon as he left to come here the first time and only just found out."

"What? How?"

"Apparently, Em, the young girl, has a fancy lawyer for a father and he got her out, plus the others, the moment he heard about it. Durham said they couldn't keep them so they'd been let go. He said because I and Young Dave had been let out, they couldn't hold his daughter or the others, and they had no choice, apparently. What a mess. But it means they are still suspects, and could have got back here and planted the crystal ball."

"This is beyond ridiculous. They released murder suspects."

"But he's right. They let me and Young Dave go pretty quickly. And the others were in the garden together, so if they had alibis that said they were together so couldn't have killed Sylvester, then they had to be released. And now, as far as the police are concerned, Em's father was right. It was an accident, and that's that. Come on, let's have that cuppa now. I'm reeling, and if it isn't tea it'll be a pint."

Seemingly done with the trail of clues, Harlow hopped from the tree onto my shoulder and lay down; I could feel his little fast-beating heart vibrating in my ear as he began to snore. Poor guy had got entangled in a very busy day, so he deserved a rest. I think I did too.

"Everything alright over there?" asked a voice from the other side of the fence.

I rolled my eyes at Charlie, who shook her head, not understanding, then I mouthed a silent, "It's the neighbour," and she nodded, realising it was the man I'd told her about many times but she'd never met. After a bit of scrabbling about, a head of thick, dark brown, curly hair appeared, then the slim, suntanned face of Joe, Aunty Clem's relatively new neighbour.

"Hi. Joe, this is my wife, Charlie. Charlie, this is Joe. I may have mentioned him."

"Hope it was all bad," he laughed, rubbing at his long beard. He liked to keep it that way for his reenactment weekends, where they'd dress up in armour and run around brandishing spears and swords and sweating under their chainmail, pretending to be Cavaliers or sometimes Vikings. He'd bored me to tears with the history of so many battles I couldn't keep track, but he never seemed to notice.

"Lovely to meet you. You okay over there? How's Clem? I had the police around earlier, saying there'd been an explosion. First I knew about it. I was in my workshop all morning with my headphones on, finalising our next meet-up this Sunday and didn't hear a thing. I've been trying to catch you, but didn't want to intrude."

"Everything's fine. Or, at least Clem is. She had a fall and broke her arm, but is okay now."

"And there was a body? Was it murder?" he asked, eyes wide, checking out the garden.

"Yes, it was. Someone got killed in the garden."

"Lucas, it was not murder. Just an unfortunate accident, Joe," said Charlie, shaking her head at me. "A man had an accident because the attic blew up. A leaky gas pipe, but everything's fine now."

"Oh, okay." Joe sounded disappointed as he lived for make-believe killing and the real thing would be very exciting, I supposed. "What happened to the poor guy?"

"We aren't quite sure, but the police are looking into it. You didn't hear anything? The explosion?"

"Nope, nothing. The police told me and I was going to come around later to check on Clem, but if she's in the hospital I guess I'll wait until she's out. You need anything?"

"No thanks. Unless you can fix arms."

"Afraid not. I have a ton of tools and what have you, though. I'm a carpenter, so I'm handy with wood if you need a hand fixing the attic."

"That's very sweet," said Charlie.

"We have to wait for the insurance company to inspect it, I think," I told him, itching to get away before he began telling us what his next reenactment might entail.

Joe climbed higher on his stepladder, and something rattled, then it was obvious he was wearing chainmail when his shoulders appeared.

"What's that?" asked Charlie, making a fatal mistake. I groaned.

"Ah, we're doing the Civil War on Sunday," he beamed, pleased to have someone to bore. "We get to use pikes and I have these amazingly realistic helmets and we even have real crossbows. Not loaded ones, obviously." He glanced at the garden, clearly trying to see if there were any remains of the body, "They took him away already?" he asked, perplexed.

"Yes, they were very thorough and very fast," said Charlie.

"Oh, shame. But that's good. Don't want to mess up the garden. Now, where was I?"

Taking advantage of him losing his train of thought, I said, "Sorry, but we have to go. We're off to visit Clem."

"Give her my best. Tell her I'll pop in. Maybe Monday as I won't intrude tomorrow and I'm out all day Sunday. Did you know that during the Civil War they actually had real—"

"Sorry, but we're already late." I took Charlie's arm and led her away before we got stuck for hours.

We trundled back up the garden, gasping with the heat after the lovely shade, and closed the kitchen door, grateful for the cool interior of the house.

"What was that all about?"

"I told you. He's one of those obsessives about ancient history. One week he's a Viking, the next he's pretending to be in World War One and jumping in muddy trenches in a field somewhere, and now he's doing the Civil War. He has a ton of gear all over the house and piles of the stuff in his workshop where he actually makes some of it, and will regale you with a blow by blow account of the latest reenactment if you give him half the chance."

"He seems nice."

"He is. Joe's lovely, but you have to be in the mood for it. And right now, I'm not. Sorry if I was brusque, but I couldn't face it."

Young Dave put the kettle on and rinsed out the mugs while Charlie checked the secret cupboard for the best biscuits— we all deserved a treat. I left them to it and wandered back out into the hall, then found myself drawn back to the attic, mindful of any traps on the way, my nerves jangling.

I surveyed the room, wondering if there was anything I'd missed, but had no clue what was meant to be here, and where, so gave it up as a lost cause. We'd have to clean up the mess, but I figured that was best left until Aunty returned, just in case we binned something she thought could be salvaged. The roof could wait a few days, as there was no sign of rain, and I inexplicably found myself over by the shelves, the "wand" with my name literally on it somehow clutched in my hand.

Harlow stirred to get himself more comfortable, then draped his tail over my shoulder, tiny little claws gripping the strap of my dungarees. Chuckling to myself, I nevertheless grabbed the box with Aunty's spellbook inside and wandered back downstairs. Sighing, I slumped onto the sofa then removed the book. I wasn't sure why, but I felt compelled to look inside, and with growing consternation, I read through the endless neat lines of spells for all kinds of things.

I stopped at one that caught my eye, and read it aloud. "To make my day brighter, make this heavy item lighter!" I truly felt let down when nothing happened, but then, of course, I wasn't holding anything. Casting nervous glances at the door in case I was caught, I picked up the weighty box and repeated the "spell." Nothing.

"Maybe I need to use the wand. Do wizards have wands? Shouldn't it be a staff?" I mused, before whispering, "Lucas, you muppet, what are you playing at?" Feeling like a first-class idiot, I balanced the box on one hand, then after a deep breath, and focusing on the warm wood in my hand, I repeated, "To make my day brighter, make this heavy item lighter."

Instantly, the wand grew dangerously hot and I nearly dropped it, but I gripped tight, held my nerve, and gasped as the spark I thought I'd seen before winked in and out of existence almost too fast to see. The box suddenly felt very light. So light in fact, that I turned my arm to get a feel for it and it clattered to the table.

"What was that?" asked Charlie, rushing in, panicked.

"You are not going to believe this!" I gasped, staring at first the wand, then the box suspiciously.

"Believe what? Is that the spellbook? Oh, cool, lemme see."

"What's going on?" asked Young Dave as he came in right behind Charlie.

"I... I just did a spell. I don't know why, but I went and got the wand, and I looked in the book, then I did one. I did a spell! It was real magic! Unbelievable!"

"Careful," warned Charlie with a chuckle. "Any more explanation marks and you'll get arrested for punctuation crime."

"Sorry, but it's true. Watch."

I felt for the inner connection with the wand, and as the wood warmed, I repeated yet again, "To make my day brighter, make this heavy item lighter." The wand sparked, the fizz over in the blink of an eye, and the box felt as light as a feather. I beamed at them both, but they just stared at me, nonplussed.

"What's meant to be happening?" asked Charlie.

"The box is lighter," I grinned. "Feel it."

The moment I handed it to Charlie, I felt the full weight return, and she took it with a frown. "Feels like a box," she shrugged. "You feeling okay? I know it's been a crazy day. Maybe you need a lie down. Young Dave, can you bring the tea in? I think Lucas needs an extra sugar."

"And we have the best biscuits too," he beamed, then shook his head as he looked at me in sympathy, like I was losing the plot or something.

"Lucas, what was that all about?" she whispered. "Now isn't the time to be messing around. It's in bad taste."

"Honestly, the wand and spell really worked. Didn't you see the spark at the tip?"

"Um, no, not that I was looking. You aren't fooling around?"

"I swear I'm not. I think Aunty Clem's been holding out on me all these years. She's not just an elderly lady looking for company. This stuff is real."

"Okay, that's it. You need to put your feet up and have a nap. You're overwhelmed, and I hadn't thought about it, but I think you might be in shock. This has been too much for you, and it's brought up too many memories of your army days. You spent so long trying to get over it, and you did so well, so I think you need to just rest up."

"Maybe you're right," I mumbled, suddenly feeling beyond tired. Why was I so sleepy all of a sudden? It wasn't the shock of the day though, I knew that much. I had gotten over what happened in the army, I knew that with certainty. This was just exhaustion because of worry, wasn't it?

Before I knew what was happening, Charlie had lifted my legs, made me lie down, and I sank into a deep, peculiar sleep.

What felt like minutes later, I yawned and stretched out, feeling disorientated but without a care in the world. A familiar sound slowly sank into my consciousness, and when I sniffed, I knew I was right. Without opening my eyes, I said, "You better not be making it streaky."

"As if!" grunted Young Dave, then continued his work.

I opened my eyes and spun so I was sitting, then watched my apprentice go up and down the wall with the roller. He was learning. His movements were smooth and regular, working from left to right as we'd discussed, always considering the predominant light source so if there were even the faintest trace of lines from the roller edges, they wouldn't be visible. It was all about the details.

The roller was loaded perfectly, and he got a good three strips before he expertly collected more paint from the tray, rolled off the excess, then got back to work.

"It's looking good. Just got started?"

Young Dave turned to me, frowning. "Nope, this is the last wall. And I've already done the woodwork. Mate, you've been out for almost two hours. I got bored hanging around, so figured I'd get started and you'd wake up. Fancy a cuppa? Your last one went stone cold."

"That'd be lovely."

"Then go make it. I'm busy." Young Dave winked, then whistled while he worked.

I noted the wand and box on the table, and shook my head to clear away a dream I'd had about reading a spell and the wand fizzing. Was it a dream? Suddenly, everything came rushing back to me, and I slumped back onto the sofa, my head pounding. Had that truly been real? I'd performed a spell? What happened then? I was suddenly exhausted, and Charlie lifted my legs up and I'd just gone to sleep.

I was overly tired, that must be it. Maybe she'd been right and I was in shock. After all, it was one helluva day. Bodies and explosions and grumpy detectives and crystal balls and trip wires. Trip strings, I reminded myself. And let's not forget the squirrel.

"Um, Young Dave?" I ventured cautiously.

"Yes mate?"

"Don't suppose there was a squirrel hanging about, was there? You didn't by chance catch one when the attic blew?" I held my breath nervously as Young Dave looked at me funny. Maybe I'd had a breakdown, the body taking me right back to a dusty desert with half a dozen men in various pieces strewn around me, my ears ringing, my body numb, not sure if I was alive or in Hell.

Young Dave's face brightened, and he said, "You mean Harlow? Course I remember. He's in the kitchen with Charlie. She nipped home to get the stuff for dinner, so is peeling potatoes. Said she'd make a start before we visit Clem, then we can eat when we get back here."

"Oh, wow, that's a relief. Thought I was going loopy there for a moment. Um, why are we eating here?"

"We figured we should stay over. Keep Harlow company kind of thing. And, er, just in case anything else crops up. You know, like clues," he whispered, glancing around like the walls might have ears.

"Oh, right."

"And because we thought you were going loopy, so figured we shouldn't let you get in a car."

"You what!? Cheeky bugger. I'm fine. I was just tired, that's all."

"If you say so, boss. But look, Lucas, that wasn't funny earlier with the magic thing. Bit insensitive, you know. Time and place, and all that."

"For a young lad, you're very grown up at times. I appreciate the sentiment, and I appreciate you looking out for Clem and me. You're a good lad."

"One who deserves a pay rise. Apprentice wages suck, and I want to get a PS4."

"But you've got all the other ones!"

"Yeah, but 4 is better than 3. And besides, I want to get my own place soon. Be independent."

"We'll see. Finish the wall, and I'll make the tea." I rose, then paused at the door and turned. "You're doing a good job, and thanks. I know today isn't the day to be decorating, but I know Clem will appreciate it."

"She will." Young Dave nodded. "Especially when she sees how the professionals do it." He winked, then loaded up the roller.

Chapter 8

The doorbell rang as I left the living room, so I rubbed my face, took a quick glance in the mirror, then hurriedly looked away, aghast with what I was confronted with, before peering through the peephole. My spirits lifted immediately, and I opened the door and smiled warmly at Frank.

"How's it going?" he asked with a friendly smile but a knowing nod.

"I've had better days, Frank. Much better."

"You look exhausted. You should take a nap."

"I just had one. That's why I look so..."

"Creased?" he suggested, eyes twinkling. Frank adjusted his oil-stained flat cap, ran his hands down his blue mechanic's overalls, and kicked at the step with steel toe-capped boots so well-worn the leather was gone from the toes, revealing the shiny metal underneath. The deeply etched lines of his face meant he seemed to be permanently smiling, and in truth he usually was. Never happier than when in the inspection pit at his garage, studying the undersides of vehicles with his light, Frank had been in the game for over fifty years and showed no signs of slowing down.

He'd been the family mechanic as long as I could remember, and a family friend. He and Aunty Clem were close, and although she didn't drive, Frank would always mend any mechanical item that needed fixing, and he often popped in for a cuppa and a chat. One thing he adored as much as motors was gossip, and between them Aunty and Frank knew just about everything about everyone.

"That bad, eh?" I sighed, stepping aside so he could enter.

"Just messing with you, lad," he chuckled as he slipped off his boots then removed his cap and ran thick fingers through short, steel-grey hair. "That where it happened, eh?" he asked, walking over to the stairs.

"That's where she was tripped," I said, joining him.

Frank turned to me and asked, "So you don't think it was an accident either," raising his eyebrows.

"No. Do you?"

"Course not. Lucas, your aunty is the fittest woman over seventy I know. Fitter than most youngsters. How many times has she gone up and down those stairs over the years? I can't even imagine. And has she ever once slipped or fallen? No, don't answer, because we know she never has."

"We found something," I said, then went on to explain about the nails and string before showing him.

"It definitely looks like someone has it in for her. But why? She's always so nice to everyone. And her group, her coven, what have they got to say about it?"

"I haven't spoken to them yet. But they've been released from questioning and everything about this just stinks." I explained the whole sorry mess to him, feeling better for getting it off my chest, but still reeling over the wand incident. My hand tingled, like the after-effects of stinging nettles, and I wondered if I should tell Frank about it.

"So murder suspects are released within hours? That's madness. And then a convenient crystal ball shows up in the garden so they can just close this case before it's even opened? Why would they do that?"

"Because they don't want the fuss. They want this hushed up and they want it solved because friends of my uncle still have a say so they want Clem to be spared any embarrassment."

"But you don't rush something like this. A man is dead."

"Yes, but if it was an accident, I suppose they want it finished with. It did happen on her property, and the attic is an issue, so they don't want Aunty to be worried."

"Makes sense," he said, scratching his head again. "Poor Clem. I know she has a lot of respect in this town, so I understand where the police are coming from. They don't want it getting into the papers that her house was the scene of a murder if it wasn't, so putting it down as an unfortunate accident makes sense. But you and me both know this isn't true, don't we?"

"I do, but I'm surprised you're so sure of it. It could just be a series of regrettable coincidences, you know?"

"With all this magic whizzing about? I don't think so."

I stepped back, shocked, not sure I even heard him right. "You believe?"

"In magic? Of course. Don't you?"

"Um, not really, no. At least, I didn't. Now I'm not so sure. But you're a mechanic. You understand machines. I'm surprised you think stuff like this could be real."

"I'm an old man, and I've been around. I've seen it all, and I've known Clem since I was a very young lad. When she started getting into this stuff again, I knew she'd make a great witch. Bit late for her, but she got right into it and is a natural. I'm shocked you're dubious."

"It's magic, Frank," I said. "Make believe. I thought it was just a bit of fun for Clem. An interest in the occult and the supernatural, not actual real magic."

"What constitutes real magic? This is a strange world, a true miracle, so it's all magical. Waving a wand or reading a spell doesn't seem that far-fetched to me. If I were you, I'd focus on the coven. Stands to reason it's one of them, right?"

"That's what I assumed. But after the day I've had, I'm not sure of anything now. I think I might have done a spell."

"That's the spirit," he laughed, slapping me on the back. "Tell Clem I was asking about her, and I'll pop in to see her when she gets home. I assume that's tomorrow?"

"Hopefully."

"Great, and don't let the police push you around. Find out who's trying to kill her, and make sure you get proof."

"You think they're trying to murder her?" I asked, stunned by his whole attitude. "And what's this about Clem being interested in the paranormal when she was young?"

"Course. Now you need to figure out why. Witches and wizards can be a cutthroat lot, so watch your back, and don't take any chances. As to your aunt's past, that isn't for me to discuss. Here are the keys." Frank fished around in his pocket, then dangled the keys as I reached for them. "I've got the lads waiting for me outside to give me a lift back to the yard."

"Great. Thanks so much."

"Change your oil regularly, or bring it in for me to do. You need to look after that vehicle. The knocking sound is sorted, and it won't cost much. I'll send you the bill. But take care."

"Of the car, or myself?"

"Both." Frank released the keys, and for a moment I could have sworn they hovered, before they landed silently in my palm, the tingle increasing as they seemed to nestle tight. I gasped, and as our eyes met, Frank winked.

"Wait! Did you just do something?"

"We all have our gifts, Lucas. I'm just a mechanic and I stick to that, but like I said, I've been around a long time. I have the touch, you know that. I can fix anything. I see what needs doing and I fix it. You understand? I *see* it. I *know*. There's magic in us all."

Frank slipped into his boots, then waved over his shoulder as he whistled his way down the path. I was left standing at the door, reeling.

Could this day get any more weird? Was I losing my marbles? Since when did everyone believe in the paranormal and that there were gifted amongst us?

Harlow studied me from the bottom step, as if expecting me to do something. What was I meant to be doing? I couldn't think straight, the lethargy not shaken after such an extended nap. Tea, that was it. A lovely cuppa. That'd sort me right out.

"You didn't have to go to all this trouble," I told Charlie as I entered the kitchen, noting the pots and pans, the mountain of peeled potatoes, and the sausages still in the paper from the butchers.

"It's no trouble." Charlie smiled and I felt better instantly. "You know I enjoy cooking. It's relaxing."

"I find it the opposite."

"That's why I cook and you wash up. A team."

"A team," I agreed.

"Feel better after your nap? More like full night of sleep?" she asked, smiling.

"Not really," I grumbled. "Look, about earlier."

"It's okay. You were obviously exhausted. It's not surprising. This has been a crazy day and you're worried about Clem. But you were acting very silly. Pretending to do magic? What got into you?"

"Charlie, that's just the thing. I wasn't messing around. I swear it. I felt something, and my hand still tingles now. Do you think it looks red?" I held out my hand for her to see, so she put down the potato peeler, wiped her hands on a tea towel, and looked at my hand, then at me.

"Maybe, but you've been doing stuff. Nothing unusual. You weren't messing around? You think something happened?"

"I know it did. And then I was exhausted, tired like I never get. You know I can manage on just a few hours. That wasn't normal for me to crash out for two hours. I never do."

"You don't," she admitted. "Doesn't make you a wizard just because you had a nap though," she teased.

"It might. I think wizards sleep a lot. Maybe this is why. The effort takes it out of you. And Frank just dropped the van off, and he said he believes. He also thinks someone's out to get Clem. Reckons it's to do with the coven. And when he handed me the keys, they, er, they floated. I know it sounds daft, it does to my ears, but I don't know what else to do. I trust you more than anyone else, and you're my wife. I don't want to hide things from you, but this is getting worrying. I think I might be losing my mind. I don't know what to do."

Charlie took my hands in hers. They were cold, and soft, and more comforting than I could ever hope to explain to her. "It's okay. You aren't losing your marbles. If you say something happened with the wand and spellbook then I believe you. We shouldn't have been so dismissive. I'm sorry."

"But I do sound crazy, right?" I asked, my shoulders relaxing. I hadn't realised how tense I was.

"A little. Maybe the best thing is to try again? Do you want to? Show us your trick? Sorry, I don't mean trick. I mean spell. Come on, the potatoes are peeled. I just need to pop them in some water then I'm done. We should go and visit Clem soon."

"Yes, that would be great. I'm famished, but I can wait. Thanks for doing this. You sure you don't mind staying over tonight? I appreciate you thinking of it."

"I don't mind. In fact, it's for the best. We can start sorting out the mess and look after the place. Plus, something's definitely going on, and we need to find out what."

"You mean it? You don't think we should back off?"

"No, I do not." Charlie got that fierce look in her eyes when her mind was made up. She was determined, and nothing would sway her now. I loved that about her.

"Good, because neither do I."

Charlie ran water into the pan, then put a lid on it and removed her apron.

Feeling nervous, which was unsettling, we returned to the living room where Young Dave was clearing things away.

"You did a great job. Thanks for finishing up."

"No problem. I just need to clean my brushes then we should go visit Clem."

"We will, but first I'm, er, going to try that spell again. Don't laugh," I warned them both. "I'm feeling foolish enough already, but I've got this feeling in my gut about it, and I'm determined to know for certain before we visit Clem. I'm sure she'll have plenty to say about this, so I want to be prepared."

"We won't laugh, but you really weren't kidding?" asked Young Dave, carefully placing his brush down on the tray.

"I'm deadly serious."

"Bad choice of words," grimaced Charlie.

"Sorry." I opened the book and flicked through the pages, trying to remain focused as Charlie and Young Dave scrunched up beside me to read the spells.

"How about that one?" asked Young Dave as he jabbed a finger at the page.

"Careful! Don't get paint on it. Clem will have a fit."

"That would be awesome if it works. Give it a go."

"Okay, but we're using your brushes. I'm not risking mine."

"Suit yourself. Wait a mo." Young Dave sprang from the sofa, grabbed a brush covered in white satin, then placed it on a clean spare painter's pot, of which we had many.

I picked up the wand, felt the warmth in the wood just like before, and emptied my mind of everything apart from the words on the page. With a nod from Charlie, her face a combination of doubt yet anticipation, I read, "Don't be mean, make this brush clean." I tapped the wand on the wooden handle of Young Dave's brush and a spark flashed from the tip as the heat flared up my arm.

"Did you see that!?" gasped Charlie, eyes gleaming, cheeks flushed.

"Blimey, I saw it this time too," gushed Young Dave, leaning forward then grabbing the paintbrush. "Feels warm. And whoa, no way, mate, look at it. Lucas, you're a wizard! Wow, ha, this is incredible!" Young Dave jumped up and brandished the brush like it was his own wand, pretend zapping things.

I sank back into the sofa, feeling exhausted yet again, and even as the elation hit, the satisfaction of knowing I hadn't been imagining it, I felt my eyes closing. With a start, I snapped to attention as Young Dave asked, "Can you do the others? We can get going then."

"I haven't got the energy," I admitted. "It takes a lot out of you. I think I need another nap."

"Lucas, that was astounding," said Charlie, pecking me on the cheek. "How did you do it? And sorry for doubting you before."

"Yeah, sorry about that," said Young Dave.

"I understand. Who would think Aunty Clem was telling the truth all along?"

Harlow hopped up onto the table and began to race around the spellbook, then stopped suddenly and with a deft swipe of his paw, he flipped through several pages at once. We all peered down at the book and gasped when we read the spell.

"Don't make me tired, make me energetic and wired." The wand became almost too much to keep hold of as the tip fizzed like a demented sparkler then fizzled out just as quick. I could tell that it hadn't worked, although where I'd tapped my knee did feel remarkably energetic.

"Well?"

"Just got an excited knee now," I admitted.

"Do knees get excited?" asked Charlie.

"This one does. Right, Young Dave, you finish cleaning up. I'm going to have a wash and freshen up then we should get going. Aunty Clem has a lot of explaining to do."

"You're just going to leave after what happened?" asked Charlie, clearly astonished.

"What else should I do? Seems everyone knows about this apart from us. Even Frank the mechanic can do it. He reckons I'll be a natural."

"He believes?" asked Young Dave.

"He does. Said he knew Clem was doing it and basically admitted to me that it's how he finds the faults with cars. Uses his gift."

"But he isn't in the coven?" asked Charlie. "Why not?"

"No idea. Maybe he didn't want to join. Maybe he wasn't asked. Although they have been good friends for decades. Maybe it was his idea. He might have suggested it to Aunty so she had an interest. I didn't ask, as he surprised me so much. But he reckons the police are wrong, too, and someone's after Clem."

"Any ideas why?"

"He didn't, but I have to say, he didn't seem too shocked by any of it. Almost like he expected it."

"Another suspect!" sang Young Dave with glee.

"Don't be daft, it's Frank. Old Frank the greasy mechanic."

"The old, magical, greasy mechanic," Charlie reminded me.

"Maybe, but why would he want to hurt her? And he's not going to tell me about magic if he tried to kill her, is he?"

"Maybe it's part of his plan," said Young Dave with an armful of brushes, rollers, and trays. "See you in ten." He left to clean everything, so I folded up the sheets and checked the room looked good for tomorrow, then turned to find Charlie still on the sofa, just staring at the book.

"Think I'll be able to do it?" she asked.

"I honestly have no idea. I don't know how any of this works. But what I do know is that it's exhausting. We need to talk to Aunty Clem about this."

"And then we have the weekend to uncover who's responsible before work again on Monday. Ugh, work! I hate that job."

"Then quit. I keep telling you, it's not worth it. They make you work extra hours, they don't ever say thank you, and life's too short to spend the majority of your day being miserable. We can afford for you to take some time off. And I do keep saying you can come and work with me and Young Dave."

"That sounds nice," mused Charlie. "But it would be weird. You'd be my boss."

"Not really. We'd be a team. And we could both gang up on Young Dave."

Charlie giggled, then said, "I'll think about it. I have had just about enough of being treated with so little respect. The whole environment stinks. Literally. Whatever was I thinking deciding to be a manager at a mattress factory? All those chemicals can't be good for you."

"That's what I keep saying. Think seriously about it. Now, are you sure you're up for this? It might be dangerous. Maybe we shouldn't stay here."

"Maybe we should," pouted Charlie, hands on hips. "I can look after myself. You know that. I saw off that mugger last year, and I'm not afraid."

"You should be. I am. This is a lot more dangerous than it looks. I just know it is. And it looks dangerous as hell."

"We'll figure this out, and we'll make the place nice for Clem."

Charlie left to finish off in the kitchen, so I went to prepare for what promised to be a very interesting visit with my Aunty   Clem.

Chapter 9

Navigating the congested corridors of the chaotic hospital felt like wading through iodine-infused soup. It seemed as though everyone in town had decided to come sniff the bleach-soaked floors and play "find the ward" as they stumbled, zombie-like, up and down the green and blue corridors, poking their heads around curtains those ensconced behind seemed to believe were soundproof for some reason. It astonished me the things you heard when passing by wards rammed full of beds, as though nobody cared if everyone heard about their intimate ailments and operations in every minute, excruciating detail.

With Charlie's help, and me and Young Dave utterly dazed by the sheer volume of people, we eventually managed to locate Aunty Clem. I insisted she'd been moved, not recognising where we were, but Charlie was adamant we were in the same place as before. Although, she did admit she was as certain as me that someone had come around and switched all the signs to tell you where to go, and the ward numbers, while we'd been busy sleuthing.

"Is she alright?" asked Young Dave nervously as we stood at the foot of the hospital bed watching Aunty Clem while the other visitors played "let's shout as loud as we can because we're behind a soundproof curtain" from the other occupied beds.

"She's just tired," I whispered, hating seeing her like this. Her hair was rather a mess, and she looked pale and tired, but there was something else. She just didn't have that spark to her.

Aunty Clem always almost glowed with radiance. A seemingly unquenchable thirst for life. Always merry, never angry, she was as positive as they came and always happy to help. Now she just looked like a frail old lady in a hospital bed waiting for the end to come.

"She looks ready to croak it."

"Young Dave! She doesn't look that bad," I said.

"Stop talking about her like she isn't here," hissed Charlie, moving closer and bending then listening to her breathing.

"Oh, good, she's alive," said Charlie, smiling as her frown faded.

"You just said she didn't look that bad. Now you're checking she's breathing?" I asked.

"I can hear you, you know," said Aunty Clem as she opened her eyes and beamed at us. Her face brightened immediately, and she shifted in the bed to get more comfortable, although by the sound of the rasping sheets it wouldn't make much difference.

"Let me give you a hand," offered Charlie, and helped Clem shuffle up the bed, supported by a mountain of pillows.

"What's the news then?" asked Clem. "Did you find out anything? I spoke to the police again, that DI Durham and his partner, and they seemed convinced this has all been a misunderstanding. What's this about a crystal ball in the garden? Did you bring it with you?"

"No, we don't have it. But how many do you have?"

"Oh, gosh, loads of them. I got very carried away a few years ago when I was new to magic, and bought so many I lost track."

"We saw in the attic," said Young Dave brightly. "You have some cool stuff up there. Is that a real human skull? And what's in the jars? Will you make me a wand? Charlie too?"

"Ah, so you found yours?" Clem asked me.

"I did. At least, I assumed it was for me. What's going on? Why is there a wand with my name literally on it? And you have one too."

"I know I do," she chuckled. "There's much to talk about, but now isn't the time or the place," she whispered, checking out the other visitors.

"Shall I close the curtain?" asked Young Dave.

"They aren't soundproof," I said, shaking my head.

"Really? You sure?"

"Positive." I turned back to Aunty Clem and asked, "Why do I have a wand?"

"I made it for you. I knew you'd take an interest eventually, but I didn't want to push you into anything. Are you a believer? Did you find my book?"

"We did. Although, er, Harlow did most of the work finding things."

"Harlow?"

"The squirrel that lives out front in the tree. The red one."

"Oh, him. Yes, he's a smart fellow, but how did he find it?"

We went on to explain exactly what had been happening. About the clues, the talks with the DI, the crystal ball, and she listened without interrupting. When we'd finished, I asked, "Well?"

"We'll talk more tomorrow. But be nice to Harlow. I think he might have got a lot smarter because of the attic incident. There were, er, some very volatile things up there. He's most likely magical now."

"A magic squirrel! Please, this is getting ridiculous." The other visitors turned, so I lowered my voice and asked, "What is really going on here, Aunty? You're hiding things from us and I don't like it. You shouldn't keep things secret that are important. You never showed me the spellbook or really explained about your coven. It's all real? Magic is real? Spells and wands and smart squirrels?"

"What do you think?"

"I think I'm exhausted."

"You did a spell, didn't you?" asked Aunty, eyes dancing, colour returning to her cheeks.

"He cleaned my brush," said Young Dave. "We saw the sparks on the wand."

"On your first go? That's very impressive."

"It wasn't my first go. I made the box lighter, but the second time I tried it didn't work as well."

"That's because it takes so much energy to do a spell when you're starting out. You need to practice. But it's still draining. It's why magic's best left to the youngsters. When you get to my age, even the smallest spell leaves you shattered for hours. You need to have been doing it your whole life to be able to avoid the side effects."

"How do you know?" I asked.

"I've spoken to real witches and wizards. Lots of them. They can communicate with animals, I mean talk to them, and do incredible things. It's all rather late for me, but not for you, Lucas. You have it in your blood. I should never have turned my back on it. It's my one regret. But thank you for visiting, and telling me what you've discovered. My, what an exciting day you've had." Aunty leaned back with a sigh and sank her head deep into the pile of pillows. "We'll talk properly tomorrow. But please don't go snooping. This whole sorry incident is over with now, so let's leave it be."

"I'll come and pick you up the moment I get a call from the hospital," I promised, then gave her a kiss on the cheek.

Aunty was asleep before we'd even left the ward.

Several hours later—at least it felt that way—we emerged from the hospital, gasping as the bleach fumes stung our eyes and burned our throats. We stood beside the doors, watching the other visitors rush out, eyes streaming, sneezing, wheezing, and coughing as the germs they'd contracted began to show their effects.

"Hospitals are the worst place to be if you're ill," noted Young Dave. "They're full of disease and weird bacteria. I feel like I'm coming down with something already." He sneezed into a tissue, looked at it suspiciously, then binned it.

"Me too. And now we have to do battle with the beast," I groaned.

We each turned to confront the black behemoth of a machine designed to torture stressed visitors when the last thing on their mind was how to fathom the mysterious intricacies of yet another parking ticket machine.

"Didn't you have to pay when you arrived before?" asked Charlie. "It was easy. You popped a coin in the slot and your ticket came out. Now you do it when you leave?"

"It's so they can time it down to the second and charge you for it. Last time I used it, it took me longer to figure out what to do than I was here for. But they've changed it again."

We stood behind a flustered man muttering about apps and how was he supposed to remember his registration, and why did he have to pay by card?

He turned to us, sweating badly, eyes darting, and asked, "Can you help me out here? I can't understand what I'm supposed to do. Why can't you just pop a coin in and go home? I just want to leave," he pleaded, glancing at the machine that beeped a warning. "No, not again. Now I have to start over and go through it all again. And why are the parking machines different everywhere you go? It's like learning a new language every time you park your car."

We spent a brain-taxing ten minutes trying to figure it out, the queue behind us getting longer and louder. At least we knew what to do when it was our turn, so we finally got our ticket and once we were in the car we joined the long line of stationary vehicles trying to escape this place of torture.

Once clear of the line of coughing and spluttering drivers, the road was quiet and we were home in mere minutes. It was only as Charlie pulled up to Aunty's that I wondered why on earth we bothered driving when a pleasant stroll would have been much better for both our legs and bank balance.

Harlow called out a hearty greeting then came down the tree headfirst before hopping onto my shoulder.

"Hey there, little buddy. Did you miss us?"

Harlow gave a single grunt in return, and I swear it sounded like he was talking. "You did? We missed you too," I laughed, feeling calmer with his warm body so close.

"He definitely likes you," noted Charlie. "What's going to happen when we leave?"

"Guess he'll go back to living in the tree and doing what squirrels do best."

"If you make a lame joke about nuts, we're getting a divorce."

"As if I would," I said seriously, turning away as my smile threatened to break loose.

While Charlie went to fix dinner, Young Dave and I cleared away all signs of our work from the living room and loaded everything into my van. Charlie would be relieved she didn't have to ferry me around, and I hated to admit it but it felt awesome to have my old faithful back, the smell of paint and turpentine as familiar as my own hands.

Young Dave didn't complain as we removed the debris from the front, loading glass into the bin, collecting the wood and tiles and salvaging what we could. In less than an hour, the garden was looking as good as new, although my pruning technique for the damaged roses might have been a little less than the perfection Aunty Clem insisted on.

Next we went up into the attic, but decided to just sweep up the glass and put the damaged paraphernalia on one of the benches rather than risk Clem's ire for throwing out something she thought of as valuable or important. Just in case it rained, although the forecast was good, we fixed a tarp under the tiles and draped it down over the window before stapling it in place. It made the room feel gloomy and sinister, much more like a witch's den than ever, and we hurried out into the light, laughing at ourselves as we shivered. Harlow remained with us the whole time, either chattering away or watching, but there were no more clues to be found and little to do apart from mull over what had transpired and try to make some sense of it.

But that was the thing. None of it made any sense. We needed more answers from Aunty Clem, but that would have to wait until tomorrow. Thankfully, we were drawn from chores by Charlie calling us for dinner, so with anticipation building—we were simple men at heart—we dashed down the stairs, then gasped as we came to a halt on the half landing and looked at each other with concern, before taking the next flight slowly, mindful of tripping.

Once we felt safe, we hurried into the kitchen to find Charlie dishing up steaming mounds of fluffy mashed potatoes with three sausages each sticking out—Desperate Dan would have been proud.

"Sit," ordered Charlie, beaming at us, always proud when her hard work was appreciated.

We didn't need telling twice, then both shot up and washed our hands before resuming our seats and clapping as Charlie poured thick, unctuous onion gravy over the top.

"Looks amazing," sighed Young Dave.

"Sure does. Thank you, Charlie. Don't know what I'd do without you."

"Eat a lot of Pot Noodles," she chuckled.

"This is awesome," mumbled Young Dave, before putting his hand in front of his mouth, knowing Charlie was a stickler for manners. He swallowed, then grinned at her and added, "Thanks for letting me hang out with you guys and to stay over. It'll be fun, right?"

"I'm not so sure about the fun part," I said, keen to tuck in. "But we like having you around. You're a good lad."

"We do," agreed Charlie. "Are things any better at home?"

"No, just the same, or maybe a little worse. I try to stay out of it. Dad'll be back tonight, then hitting the booze hard. Mum will be giving him grief, complaining about having to make him dinner even though she won't let either of us help, and doesn't even cook for me even though I pay my way. She'll just sit there, glaring at him, and stewing while he slowly sinks into oblivion in front of the TV." Young Dave bit a sausage in half, his face brightening.

"It must be difficult. Was it always like this?" asked Charlie.

"Pretty much. Same thing year in, year out. Only change has been what Dad drinks and how little Mum does around the house. I think she's depressed. It isn't normal to mope around like that and not even get dressed if she's off work. She hardly cleans, forgets to eat, and usually forgets to make dinner. But yes, I know

I'm a grown-up and can tend for myself, cook my own meals, and that's what I mostly do, but still..."

"We get it. And let's be honest, Young Dave, you're almost a man at seventeen, but your parents should be looking after you, as that's what they're supposed to do. You're doing great, and things might change. Maybe your mum is poorly. Try to understand that life is hard for some people and they find it very difficult to cope. Main thing is don't let it get you down. You're a bright lad with a promising future ahead of you. Your work is top-notch, you're conscientious, even if you never get here on time, and soon you'll be benching as much as me."

"In your dreams!" laughed Young Dave. "I bench more than you now. How many chin-ups can you do?"

"Twenty."

"Liar."

We laughed and joked our way through the rest of dinner, keeping the tone light. There was no point going over Young Dave's home life too deeply. There was nothing we could do beyond what we already did, and that was to look out for the lad. But it was obvious he preferred being with us than his parents, and him staying over tonight was a clear sign things were deteriorating for him. I doubted he'd last much longer before trying to move out, but rents were sky-high, bills had almost doubled in the last year, and the truth was he had no experience of what it actually took to run your own household. He was, even though he might have felt different, still a kid.

With dinner over, and our bellies full, Young Dave and I cleaned up the kitchen while Charlie relaxed in the garden. It was a lovely evening and a shame to waste it, so once we were done, we took coffee outside and joined Charlie at the white cast iron table and chairs situated under an arbour at the side of the garden that afforded wonderful views of the herbaceous borders in full bloom. Bees buzzed, birds sang, and Harlow joined us then curled up on Charlie's lap, much to her delight.

"What's the plan, then?" asked Young Dave casually.

"How'd you mean?" I asked.

"I mean, when are we going to start asking people questions?" Charlie and I exchanged a look, nonplussed; Young

Dave sighed. "Guys, come on! We have to start interviewing everyone who was here to find out who did this. And let's not forget that Lucas here is a wizard now."

"I'm not a wizard. Don't be daft. I did a spell. Wow, that sounds nutty even now. I'm not dreaming, am I? This is beyond crazy."

"No, you aren't dreaming," said Charlie, reaching forward carefully so as not to disturb Harlow and patting my knee. "You did magic, and by the sounds of it Clem had hoped you would. I'm sure she'll have plenty more to say about this tomorrow."

"I hope so, because she didn't exactly give us many answers. She also wants us to leave it alone and not interfere. Although, as far as everyone else is concerned, this is all over."

"And what about finding the murderer?" asked Young Dave.

"I honestly don't know what to do," I admitted. "Nothing like this has ever happened before."

"You were in the army," he said, like that explained everything.

"Yes, but I wasn't a detective. I went to war in-between mostly not going to war. It's not the same thing."

"No, but you know people. You're good at reading them."

"You are," agreed Charlie. "You are very good at reading body language and solving problems for people. You always have been."

"Really?"

"Yes, really. My husband is an amateur wizard detective now," said Charlie, smiling at me and winking.

"That's right," agreed Young Dave hurriedly, leg twitching as his eyes sparkled. "We need to solve this so Clem's safe.

I put my coffee down, looked to them both, then smiled as I said, "Then I suppose I better come up with a plan."

"Yes!" Young Dave fist-pumped the air, causing Harlow to spring awake then jump onto the grass and check for danger.

"Calm down," laughed Charlie.

"Can we bring the squirrel?" asked Young Dave.

"I'm not sure we'll have a choice," I said, as Harlow landed on my shoulder and curled up.

Chapter 10

We decided to go and visit Mike the metalhead. Mostly because I knew he was the closest, having given him a lift home once when his car wouldn't start. I didn't have his phone number, and we couldn't find where Aunty kept her contacts—they were most likely all on her phone now, as she'd embraced technology to some degree and ditched the reams of paper with addresses and phone numbers years ago—so we'd have to just show up and hope he was home.

Charlie insisted we go in her Mini Cooper as she hated the smell of my van, so we piled in with Harlow hopping into the back with Young Dave, seemingly keen to be part of the gang.

"Is nobody else finding it strange to have a squirrel in the car?" I asked.

"People take dogs all the time," noted Young Dave, patting Harlow's head.

"Yes, they do. But they are dogs, not squirrels. What if he needs a pee? How will we know?"

"Young Dave will have a wet leg," laughed Charlie as she started the car and we headed south for several miles.

It wasn't long before we pulled up outside a nondescript semi-detached in the heart of suburbia. Mike's Subaru and a nice Mercedes were parked outside the double garage, the neat front lawn lined with petunias.

"He lives here?" asked Charlie.

"This is where I brought him. I don't even know if he's married or with someone or what the deal is. I never asked and he didn't say. We mostly chatted about music."

"Then let's find out," said Young Dave. He reached to open the door, then paused and said, "What if he is the murderer? Isn't this a bit dangerous?"

"He's not going to just kill us all," I said. "And besides, we have our guard squirrel to protect us, right, Harlow?" I winked at Harlow who sat upright on his haunches and let loose with a tirade of noise, gesturing with his tiny paws. "See, he'll protect us."

"Guys, be serious. Maybe this isn't such a good idea."

"Maybe you're right," I agreed. I turned to Charlie and asked, "Should we go home? We could be getting in way too deep here. We don't know what we're dealing with, and the death was pretty brutal. Mike's a big guy. What would we do if he tried something? I think we should go home. I couldn't live with myself if something happened to you."

"Nothing will happen. There are three of us and just one of him. And anyway, look, we don't have to worry." Charlie pointed out of the window and we watched as Mike trailed behind a couple in their sixties. He looked like a sulky teenager as he tugged on the lead of a chihuahua that was peeing against the Mercedes' wheel.

The man, who I assumed was Mike's father judging by the similarities in size and features, turned and started berating the dog, so Mike tugged harder and told the dog off. The smug pooch lowered its leg after a final spray then skipped forward as they all entered the property.

"He lives with his folks?" asked Charlie. "He's a bit old for that, isn't he?"

"Maybe he looks after them? Or maybe he can't afford rent. Or maybe he likes it here," I said with a shrug.

"Or maybe he's lazy and doesn't have a job," said Young Dave.

"Don't be so quick to judge. Maybe he wants a job but can't get one, or maybe there's something else going on. But one thing's for sure, we don't have to worry about him murdering us all. Doubt he's going to do that with his parents around."

"Unless they're all in on it and jump us the minute we ring the doorbell," said Young Dave brightly.

"We can live in hope," I grumbled as I opened the door and stepped out into the warm evening air.

The others joined me, with Harlow racing around us, clearly not a fan of car journeys.

Young Dave glanced back at us, then squared his shoulders, looking like a scared rabbit, but nevertheless he rang the doorbell then jumped back by our side as the door was yanked open.

Mike's eyes widened when he saw us, then he glanced back into the house before coming outside and pulling the door closed behind him.

"What are you doing here?" he hissed, glaring at me.

"Why are you so angry?" I asked.

"Me? Oh, I don't know, maybe because I got dragged down to the police station and asked a load of questions by the detectives."

"That's not our fault, is it? Why are you blaming us?"

"I'm not blaming you, but it was awful. They had me there for ages, asking the same questions over and over, and it was just the worst. Then I had to come and explain to my parents what happened, as the police wanted to talk to them, and they had to go through what happened before I left to meet Clem and the others this morning and there was all this weirdness because of our coven. Nobody else understands, and they refuse to admit we aren't just a joke. And now you're here, to make fun of me like everyone else, and I suppose you think I had something to do with it. Well?" Mike tried to suck in his large belly and puff out his chest to intimidate us, but I wasn't afraid of him, and I realised I wasn't feeling much of anything now I was actually doing something.

The army training kicked in like it hadn't for years, and I was cool and calm, un-flustered and letting my awareness expand, taking in his mannerisms, his facial movements, his body language. Reading telltale signs and yet prepared for any eventuality. It was actually a little frightening knowing I still had all this inside when I thought I'd put it all behind me a long time ago.

Coolly, I studied Mike in his incongruous Spice Girls T-shirt, his tattoos, all the rings, and his thick army surplus shorts, then asked, "Can we come in? We'd like to ask you a few questions."

"I'm done with answering questions today. I'm sick of it." Mike turned to go back inside, but I put a hand to his arm. Not roughly, but enough to show I wouldn't back down.

"And I'm not too happy about someone trying to kill my aunt or that someone did murder Sylvester. Aren't you concerned? One of your coven is a killer. The attic blew up, although that might have just been Aunty Clem," I conceded.

Mike deflated under my hard stare and insistent tone. "Fine. But you've got this all wrong. I already know they found what killed poor Sylvester, and that Clem just took a dive down the stairs. She should know better than to mix all those chemicals together. Anything could have happened."

"Mike, anything did happen. You were there, and you heard Clem say it wasn't a trip. You were looking after her. She appreciates that, we all do, but we need answers."

"You really think it wasn't all just an unfortunate accident?" He held my gaze and I shook my head. "Okay, but take your shoes off, and don't mention a word of this to my folks. They're already in a sour mood after the questioning, and they hate me hanging with the coven as it is. This was the final straw for them. They're always on at me." Mike opened the front door. Charlie and I exchanged a puzzled look, not knowing what to make of this. Mike was acting like a kid, not a grown man of our age.

We dutifully removed our shoes in the narrow hallway, almost gagging on the overpowering smells of polish and air freshener, then trailed after Mike into a kitchen where his father was sitting reading a newspaper and his mum was busy at the sink washing dishes. Ornaments lined the window sills, gleaming and aligned perfectly. Paperweights, vases, and several snow globes. There were also three small crystal balls. The walls were festooned with photos Mike no doubt cringed over, showing him when he was young and without long hair or tattoos. The chihuahua looked up from a bed tucked into the corner, then curled back up and went to sleep. It reminded me that I'd forgotten about Harlow.

"A few friends came by to check on me. We're going to my room."

"That stinking shed, you mean," snapped his father with a sour look at us all before burying his head in the newspaper again.

"Would your friends like a cup of tea?" asked his mum.

"Why don't you ask them?" pouted Mike.

With a tsk, she turned to us, smiled unsurely, then asked, "Tea?"

"No thanks," I said, the others shaking their heads.

"Come on, this way. Don't forget your shoes."

We retrieved our shoes, then followed Mike out of the door into the back garden, a sparse space laid to lawn with tight borders of more petunias and a large black shiplap shed taking up almost the full width of the bottom of the garden. A chair and table were outside on a mean patio, but it was obvious the garden wasn't used much, or little more than an afterthought. Sun worshippers this family were not.

"Shoes," said Mike as he used a key to unlock a large padlock.

"Why didn't we just come around the side rather than through the house?" I wondered.

"Because my folks are paranoid about security, so keep the side gate locked. It's also so they can keep tabs on me," he whined, looking petulant. I couldn't figure him out. He wasn't like this when away from his home.

We dutifully removed our shoes once more and entered a world very different to the main house. Posters of death metal bands, dark painted walls, red light from a lamp draped with muslin, a floor covered in layers of worn rugs, what looked like a sofa reclaimed from a skip, a gaming chair in front of a large TV, and a double bed rammed into the back corner made it look more like a teenager's room. Again, it was incongruous.

"You sleep here?" asked Young Dave.

"Yep. Perfect for when I want to bring the ladies home." Mike grinned, nodding to the bed.

"How come you don't have your own place?" Young Dave asked.

Mike frowned, then snapped, "Do you?"

"No, but I'm seventeen and an apprentice. What do you do for money?"

"That." Mike pointed at the gaming chair.

"You sit down?" I asked, nonplussed.

"No, gaming. I play all the nastiest, most bloodthirsty games. Live streaming, competitions, that kind of thing. My Youtube channel has over two-hundred thousand subscribers. I make plenty."

"Sweet," gushed Young Dave. "I'd love to do that."

"You'd go out of your mind," I laughed. "You like getting out and about."

"True, but I could do it part time." Young Dave turned to Mike again and asked, "So how come you live with your folks? You're in your thirties, right?"

"Yeah, well, I've been there and done that. When I broke up with the missus, which was gnarly, I moved back for a bit, just to get my head right. I just haven't got around to getting a new place. This suits me just fine. I get my meals cooked, my laundry done, and they mostly leave me alone."

"Sounds good." Young Dave ogled the chair longingly, eyes almost bugging out of his head when he spied the PS4.

I didn't believe Mike for one moment, so there was clearly something else going on here, but it was obvious that was all we'd get from him on the matter.

"Let's just get this over with," grumbled Mike with a sour look at us. "But I want you to know that I think the world of Clem, and I liked Sylvester. Miranda is a pain, but her heart's in the right place underneath all that fake posh crap. Even the newbie, Em, seems sweet. And Shirley is great. She makes me cakes. I checked on Clem and it's great she'll be home tomorrow, so I don't know what you want from me."

"What happened in the garden?" I asked. "I haven't had the chance to find out, or hear what happened to you guys. One minute you were out there, the next the second explosion happened and you rushed in saying Sylvester was dead."

"Super dead," Mike reminded me.

"Right. Super dead."

"Look, I don't really want to think about it. It was so gross. I mean, super gross."

"Then super tell us," I snapped, becoming annoyed with his attitude.

"Fine. Don't get your knickers in a twist." Mike crashed back onto his musty brown sofa and grabbed a battered takeaway cup and sucked on the straw then lifted his head and told me, "I'm sorry what happened. I like all those guys. It was the worst."

"We know it's hard, Mike, but we need to know what you saw," said Charlie. "The police have written this all off and it doesn't feel right."

"Okay, so, we were in the garden and everyone was just milling about kind of thing, and discussing the explosion and poor Clem's fall. Sylvester and Shirley were gushing over the flowers, I was talking to Em, or at least I was talking, she was just standing there, and, um, who else? Right, Miranda was being loud and obnoxious as usual, trying to act like the garden wasn't up to her high standards, then I guess we heard the explosion and someone shouted something and we all looked up and we could see smoke billowing, but there were no bits of house flying about or anything as I guess it wasn't as intense as the first explosion, and then when we looked around Sylvester was just there, super dead. It was gnarly."

"Was he still next to Shirley?"

"I don't think so. She was freaking out, grabbing at me, and everyone was just in shock. We were all by him then, I guess, staring at the body. It doesn't really compute when you see something like that, you know?"

"I know," I said, all too aware of what he meant. "There are some sights your brain just can't handle, refuses to believe are real. So you don't know if Shirley was still beside him when the explosion happened?"

"No. Could have been any of us. Apart from me," he added hurriedly, taking a nervous suck on the straw, draining the dregs like a kid. "And we were literally only out there a few seconds anyway. Then we all rushed back inside and I guess you know the rest. I think the cops are right, and this was just an accident. I know Clem's tough, but anyone can trip. Maybe there was a smaller explosion before the main ones and it put her off and she stumbled."

"Maybe," I said, shaking my head to warn the others not to tell Mike everything we'd uncovered.

Harlow appeared from somewhere and hopped up beside Mike and began gesticulating, but I didn't understand what he was trying to say, if he was trying to say anything at all.

"What's with the squirrel?" asked Mike, shifting as far from Harlow as he could.

"Harlow's been tagging along. He got knocked out, remember?"

"Course I do. You alright now, little fella?" asked Mike, fists bunching, a nervousness to his voice.

"What's wrong?" I asked.

"I'm just not a fan of squirrels. No offence," he told Harlow.

Smart fellow that he undoubtedly was, Harlow sprang onto my shoulder and nibbled my ear lobe nervously.

"What can you tell us about the abilities of yourself and the others?" asked Charlie.

"The magic stuff, you mean? All this?" Mike gestured to a wide bookcase groaning under the weight of countless books and plenty of odd items including five crystal balls arranged in order of size, several straw dolls, numerous crystals, and other things that just looked like regular rocks and pebbles.

"Yes, how good are you? And the others? Do you have a spellbook?"

"We all have one," gushed Mike, suddenly animated. He heaved off the sofa, flung his long hair behind his shoulders, and retrieved a battered, leather-bound book. He held it up, smiling, and said, "I carved the leather myself."

We each leaned in to study the decorative skull he'd embossed into the leather, and made the appropriate noises of interest.

"I've got loads of spells in here. We share them, and sometimes make our own up, but mostly it's ones we find in rare books, or hear about from others. Pretty cool, eh?"

"Very," I said. "So, how good are you at magic? Do you have a wand?"

"Course I've got a wand." Mike retrieved a chunky piece of polished ebony wood and waved the wand around. We all ducked, just in case it went off, and Harlow slid into the big front pocket of my dungarees then poked his head out.

"Careful with that!" I warned.

"What's with you guys?" Mike frowned at us, then laughed. "Oh, I get it. You thought this was like for real? Real spells and real magic? Look, I'm not dumb. It's an interest, okay? A way to get out of the house and meet people who are into this stuff the same as me. We don't go turning people into newts or making things disappear. It's fascinating, and very cool, but you know." Mike shrugged, eyes lowered, then replaced the book but kept hold of the wand.

"You mean you don't believe it's real?" asked Young Dave.

"Well, yes, and no. There's power we can harness, I'm sure of it. But it's so difficult to do. Takes decades of practice, apparently. And some are more gifted than others. I'm great at saying the spells, and I swear one time my wand began to feel a little warm. But I haven't actually done a spell that changed anything. That would be so cool, though."

We all exchanged a perplexed look, then I blurted, "But I did a spell. I read Clem's book then used the wand, and it did get hot, and the end fizzed and it worked."

Mike stared at me, mouth hanging open, and asked, "For real?"

"Lucas, what are you talking about?" asked Charlie.

"The spell. You and Young Dave were there, you saw. The tip sparkled and the brush was cleaned."

"My brush?" asked Young Dave. "When?"

Suddenly I went cold all over, and felt dizzy. I staggered to the sofa and sat, ice creeping up my spine. Had it happened again? It had been years, and there had been no hint of this returning. Was I losing my grip on reality? Imagining things? Misremembering like I had when I'd left the army and regular life just wasn't enough for me. It was so mundane. No danger, no adrenaline rush, no fear. Just brushes and rollers and white wall after white wall. I'd begun to have flashbacks, then even felt it was real, but it had lasted mere weeks and once I'd got into a routine they'd stopped. A slight case of PTSD like so many had, but mild in comparison and I thought it was all behind me.

"You alright?" asked Mike.

"Fine. I think. Just, er, felt a little light-headed."

"I think it's time for us to go," said Charlie. "Sorry about Lucas being silly like that. He wasn't making fun of you. He was just messing about, weren't you, Lucas?" Charlie nodded her head vigorously and Young Dave did the same.

"Oh, yes, just trying to lighten the mood. Imagining what it would be like to be able to do real magic. Ha, can you imagine?"

"It would be awesome," said Mike. "We all try, but none of us can actually do proper stuff like that. It might be possible, in fact I know it is, but mostly it's an interest. Look, sorry about Clem, and let her know I'll be in touch, but you guys are barking up the wrong tree. It was an accident. A shame, but there you go."

Charlie reached out and I took her hand. I walked, numb, from Mike's and it was only once we had been led back through the house and were outside and with our shoes back on that I asked, "Am I losing my mind? Did I make all that up? I thought it was real. No, it was real. I'm sure. I know myself and I'm not losing the plot."

"Of course it was real," said Young Dave. "But you should have kept quiet. Even I know that."

"He's right, but I'm sorry we put you through that. We saw you do the spell, so don't worry, you aren't going mad. But Mike shouldn't know. Good job he doesn't actually truly believe, or it could have meant trouble."

I sighed with relief. "Sorry, I didn't think. I assumed they could all actually do this now I know Clem wasn't just playing around. But I guess I was right all along and for the others, or certainly Mike, it's just an interest, not something they truly believe in."

"We don't want Mike thinking you can do what he has tried for years to do," said Charlie. "You have to keep this to yourself. It could mean trouble, and we don't know what the others are capable of. One thing we do know is that it wasn't Mike."

"Even though he has crystal balls, and his parents do? Did you see them all lined up and gleaming in the kitchen?" asked Young Dave.

"I did. But that doesn't mean they planted one in the garden," said Charlie.

"You're right, and sorry about that. I just assumed now we know this is the real deal, that they believed too. No way was it Mike. I think he was telling the truth. This set-up is not what someone who killed a coven member would live like. A shed in the garden? Lots of books but no skill? No, he's just happy to have people to hang out with who share the same interests."

"None of that means he couldn't have done it," said Young Dave. "How can you both be sure?"

"Because he's scared of squirrels," we chorused.

I chuckled, said, "Jinx," then added, "Mike's averse to blood, and scared of little animals, so I can't see him killing Sylvester. And besides, there's no way someone that large managed to sneak around the house, and with those thick fingers of his he couldn't tie a tiny knot like that on the string."

"That's dumb. Anyone could have done it," said Young Dave.

"He couldn't even do his laces. You saw that. He just left them loose, tucked them in, and had problems with the keys. His fingers are really chunky. But let's go home. It's getting on and I'm exhausted."

"Sorry to scare you like that," said Charlie, eyes full of sympathy.

"It's fine. Just panicked for a moment, but I knew deep down what happened was real. I wonder if all the others feel like Mike? We need to find out."

"And we will. But tomorrow," said Charlie.

Chapter 11

"You took your time," hissed Miranda, another coven member, as we exited the car and headed towards the foot-tapping menace.

"How could we have taken our time when we hadn't arranged to meet you? We aren't late because we never said when we'd we back, and actually we were quicker than we'd expected to be."

"Don't you take that attitude with me, Lucas Moran." Miranda got right up in my face, and wagged a finger, then seemed to remember herself and took a step back, plastered a fake smile on her even more fake-tanned face, batted her fake eyelashes, and smoothed down her tight pink vest then jiggled her skin-tight jeans so they rode higher. It was quite a show, and she took her time about it while we stood there, becoming increasingly annoyed.

"Can we please just go inside?" I sighed. "I'm beat."

"You're beat? You're beat! You haven't been dragged down to the police station and asked a thousand questions."

"Actually, I have," I said. "And so has Young Dave here. We're tired."

"And I did the decorating this afternoon," said Young Dave.

"And I don't believe we've been introduced," said Charlie, competing with Miranda for the fake smile gold medal.

Both women eyed up the other, and I knew that within a second the decision would be made if they liked each other or not. I didn't need to be a genius to guess what Charlie would think, and I knew Miranda would hate there was another pretty woman in figure-hugging faded jeans to battle against. I'd seen her in action before, and if she felt at all threatened she tried to outmanoeuvre them at every turn, believing, wrongly, that she could get the men to do her bidding just by swaying her hips.

"Miranda, this is Charlie. Charlie, this is Miranda."

"Hello," said Charlie.

"Hello. That's a very, er, comfortable looking blouse."

"Ouch!" whispered Young Dave, and I stifled a giggle.

"And you look like you're very held in and uplifted by that top. Can you breathe in those jeans?" asked Charlie sweetly, with a comeback that made the colour drain from Miranda's face.

Before this got out of hand, I opened the front door and let Harlow enter first, our own personal miniature bodyguard. He took a wide birth around the fuming Miranda, coughing as he got a whiff of her overpowering, expensive perfume. Miranda stormed in behind him, seemingly unperturbed by a squirrel in the house.

We followed her in reluctantly, but I left the front door open in the hope she wouldn't be staying long. Young Dave, smart lad that he was, made a beeline for the kitchen, leaving Charlie and I to watch as Miranda looked around the entrance hall, scowling at the plants but staring wistfully at the stairs.

"I've always loved this hall. So expansive. I'm not a fan of all the plants as the water could mark the tiles, but the stairs are just divine. Wouldn't you just love to own a staircase like this? I can see myself standing on the half landing in a nice dress, waiting to greet my guests as they arrived. It's a shame Clem won't sell. I'd love to buy it. My Aaron said we can afford it if we sell a few things, but Clem just won't see sense."

"You asked to buy the house?" I said, surprised.

"Yes. It's too large for Clem at her age. That fall goes to show she'd be better off in a bungalow. A woman her age shouldn't be messing with chemicals in her attic and almost blowing up the entire street. Maybe she'll see sense after her accident."

"What about the death? Doesn't that put you off?" asked Charlie.

"Not really." Miranda shrugged. "Might mean she'll sell for a lower price. After all, you have to declare these things when you sell and nobody will want it now. And anyway, it was just an accident. Everyone says so."

"But she isn't thinking of selling. This is where she's lived for decades. She loves it here." I couldn't imagine Aunty Clem in a bungalow. This was her home, where she belonged.

"Of course, we'd have to change a few things," continued Miranda like nobody else had spoken. "Get rid of the roses, nasty things, and redo the kitchen. It's so dated. But the light's good, and the rooms are a wonderful size, and we aren't short of money."

I wanted to shake her, and tell her to stop always boasting about money. That nobody was impressed because her husband had a good job, and it didn't make her better than anyone else. But I knew it was pointless. Miranda was always talking about how her children went to private school and the fees were more than I earned in a year, forgetting to mention that they were spoiled, badly behaved children, and very rude whenever I'd met them. Clem had said they were always like that, but Miranda let them get away with murder because she'd always given them too much and they hadn't learned the value of money. But I also got where Miranda was coming from. She was proud she'd got out of a rough council estate and made a life for herself. She lived for her kids, her home, and her husband, in that order, and just didn't know how to express herself properly.

She still drove me up the wall, though.

"What can we do for you, Miranda?" asked Charlie, rolling her eyes at me. "We've had a very intense day and Lucas needs to rest."

"What about me?" she shrieked. "Hauled off to the police station like a common criminal. Oh, it was awful. Those detectives were so mean. If it wasn't for that whatsherface new girl and her lawyer father, I'd probably be in a cell getting unspeakable things done to me. You know they all like pretty women. I'd be ravaged!"

"You were there for a few hours," I sighed, "same as everyone else. We just spoke to Mike, and were going to come see you tomorrow, but I guess we may as well get this over with now. What did you see in the garden before Sylvester was killed?"

Miranda frowned, then sighed dramatically, and with a slump of the shoulders said, "We were only out there for a moment. I think I was looking at the flowers, or something like that." She waved it away as unimportant. "Then poor Shirley screamed and I turned to see Mike beside Sylvester, babbling about him being 'super dead' or some such nonsense. Then I saw the wound and ran into the house along with everyone else."

"But did you see who he was talking to before he died?"

"Shirley, I think. Or was it Em? I can't remember. Who does? I told the detectives the same thing. What's this all about?" she demanded. "Are you accusing me? Me!"

"Nobody's accusing anyone of anything. We just want to know what happened," I said.

"It doesn't matter now anyway, because it was just a horrid accident. Clem's to blame really. Messing around with chemicals and blowing up the attic. Silly woman. I told her those crystal balls were dangerous. Now look what's happened."

"You don't have any of your own?"

"No, I'm a proper witch," she pouted. "We don't need things like that. I have my books of spells and my wand and that's all I need. Plus my crystals. They have real power. And my Tarot. I could never be without those."

"Where do you get your wands from?" I asked.

"Why?"

"I don't know," I admitted. "I just wondered."

"We make them. It's very important that you find the correct wood for your energy vibrations. You need to go and look for a branch that's the right thickness and the right wood and feel around until a connection is made. It can take years to find the right piece."

"How long did it take you?"

"Oh, I was lucky. It only took five minutes," she said smugly. "I just went into my garden and found a hazel tree and I reached out and felt the beauty in it. I got Aaron to cut it for me, and sand it, and then I made the rest myself. Want to see?" Before we could answer, Miranda fished around in her seemingly bottomless Gucci bag and pulled out her wand, brimming with pride.

"So you did most of the work, then?" I said, winking at Charlie who rolled her eyes.

"Oh yes. A wand is a very personal thing. I'm rather good with it, actually. I even know lots of spells by heart."

"I can't wait to see," said Charlie, playing along.

"Me neither."

Miranda frowned, and said, "We aren't meant to do it to show off. It should be within the coven unless it's an emergency. But I suppose this is urgent. If you say we have a nasty murderer on the loose, then I might need to use my gift. Better warm the old girl up."

"Can you find the murderer?" I asked, knowing there was zero chance of Miranda actually being able to do anything if Mike couldn't. Did she even believe like we did? I still couldn't come to terms with the fact that I did.

"Oh no, nothing like that. I'm just learning, and it takes a long time, but I can perform some very fun things. Here we go then." Miranda spread her legs, hitched up her jeans, closed her eyes, and lifted her wand. The pale wood began to shine brighter and Miranda spoke confidently as she said, "Show me the fall, now you hear my call."

She spun, and with a deft flick of the wrist zapped at the stairs. Silver light shone from the tip of her wand and bounced off the red carpet before zinging up the walls. A spectral figure of Aunty Clem suddenly appeared, then tumbled down the stairs before the image began to fade.

Charlie and I rushed over, and I dashed up as if I could save Aunty, but that wasn't what my aim was. I bent and with Charlie beside me, sure enough there was a red line of thick string strung across the step. There was no longer any doubt. It was no accident. How you would go about explaining this to the police, I had no idea, and it wasn't like it would be admissible as evidence.

Charlie and I exchanged a wide-eyed glance, utterly gobsmacked, then turned to Miranda who was at the foot of the stairs.

"Sorry it wasn't very good. It's actually a very advanced piece of magic. I'm the best at it in our coven, but not everyone knows I can do it. There are some," she pouted, "who still don't believe what we do is genuine. Like Mike, that sneak."

"That was incredible," I said, meaning it. "I have to admit, I didn't think you were going to be able to do anything at all."

"Me neither," said Charlie.

"Why? Because I boast about my house and kids and act like a dumb gold-digger? I know what I am and how I come across, but I can't help it. I don't know how else to act. This is the only place and the only few hours a week I get to be myself and truly enjoy life." Miranda hung her head and began to sob.

Charlie went to her and wrapped her arms around Miranda's shaking shoulders, wand held limp at her side.

"Hey, it's okay. You're a great witch and we're all very impressed. Thank you for showing us."

"So you believe?" she asked, dabbing at her eyes as Charlie released her.

"How could we not after seeing that? Was it what really happened? Like a replay of the past?"

"Not quite. More like a ghost, I suppose. Drawing the energy from here and letting it coalesce. Sorry, it's hard to explain and I'm not even sure I really know. Maybe part memory of the building, part looking into the past. It usually doesn't work, but my guess is it's because of the energy being so strong here."

"So we could just go into the garden and replay how Sylvester died?" asked Charlie.

"I doubt it. It's too open. Not enough things to have stored the memory. I've never got it to work outside, or anywhere else very often, but there is enough power and good vibrations here to draw on. It's a special place, which is why I wanted to buy it. But yes, I was just showing off about money again. I'm sorry." Miranda began to cry again, her thick mascara running down her cheeks.

I heard the kitchen door open and saw Young Dave poke his head out, then slam it shut when he saw what was happening. I didn't blame him.

"What was that about Mike?" I asked. "You called him a sneak."

"He is. He pretends he can do magic, but I know he can't. Just because he can't use his wand like a real man... Oh, sorry, I know how that sounded," tittered Miranda. "Yes, sorry, but he doesn't truly believe, and that means he can't harness any power. But some people just aren't that way. Wrong vibrations."

"So he hasn't seen any of you perform real magic then?"

"Of course. He's part of the coven. But he thinks it's some kind of trick. He jokes around about it sometimes, asking for our secrets. He wants it to be real, that's the thing, but deep down I know he doesn't believe."

"That's not what he told us," I said, turning to Charlie.

"He was lying! What else did he lie about? He told us he truly believed."

"Oh, don't blame him for that. He's just a poor, confused man who wants company. And I shouldn't have shown you my skills. We're sworn to secrecy. No showing off to outsiders. But you're family, so it's different. And if poor Clem is in danger, then I had to try to help. But watch out for Mike, he's a slippery one."

"In what way?"

"Just that he says one thing but means another. He doesn't always tell the truth. Not that I'm saying he killed Sylvester, and are you sure about this? The police were very insistent it was just an unfortunate series of events."

"We're sure. But don't worry about that, you just go home now and maybe have a glass of wine. It is Friday night."

"Unfortunately, every evening is Friday evening when it comes to the wine. Aaron is always away working or out dining clients, and I'm alone in that stupid big house that takes so long to clean I'm going out of my mind. Now he's got a new job and it's even worse. I may as well not even be married. Sorry, you don't want to hear about that. I promise I'll try not to be so stuck up, but I just don't seem to be able to relax and relate to people. Friends?"

"Friends," I agreed.

"Definitely," smiled Charlie, hugging Miranda.

We watched her leave, then I closed the door and we both just looked at each other, not sure what to say.

"That was..."

"Unexpected?" laughed Charlie.

"Very. Speaking of wine, shall we crack open a bottle?"

"Yes please. I thought you'd never ask."

Harlow made an appearance, then waited outside the kitchen door as if he fancied a tipple himself. I guess we'd all had a very long and difficult day, but no way was I going to deal with an inebriated squirrel. The day had been weird enough already.

Chapter 12

I tossed and turned through the night, unable to banish worry and nerves. Plus, if I'm being honest, excitement and anticipation. Aunty Clem had always insisted her coven was real, but had point-blank refused to show me any magic. She'd done Tarot, looked into her crystal ball, and read my aura, but they were all things that could be dismissed as little more than simple fun. I hadn't been a believer, so had merely taken it at face value as a nice hobby for her, and a good sign she still had a lust for life. As the years went by, I paid it hardly any mind beyond occasionally bumping into her coven when their meetings coincided with a visit.

Now everything she'd said and done held deeper meaning. And how far did this go? What could be achieved? My aunty was a witch. What about the rest of the family? What about me? How much could be accomplished? And how did any of it work anyway? What Miranda had done was truly astounding. A glimpse into the past. Could Aunty recreate the scene in the garden and we'd simply stand and watch events unfold? Miranda said it couldn't be done as there wasn't enough to hold the memory, or something like that, but maybe a more powerful witch or wizard, and I couldn't believe I was using those terms, could do it? The possibilities were endless. And rather frightening.

With thoughts whirring in my head a mile a minute, I dressed in jeans and a plain black T-shirt—both splattered in red paint, an occupational hazard—and decided to have an early start.

Very early. It was four in the morning, and although I was usually up by half five or six as I enjoyed sitting outside in the garden and listening to the birds in the summer when it was light so early, I figured I'd make the most of it and take a cuppa out into Clem's astonishingly beautiful garden and enjoy the peace.

But more than that. I wanted to use the wand and spellbook again. I couldn't get it out of my mind. I wanted to do it again. I wanted to be a wizard!

Lucas Moran, painter and general handyman, wanted to be a wizard. It sounded ridiculous, but why not? If Frank and Miranda, and even Sylvester, an accountant, could do it, then why not a painter?

With my heart beating fast, I crept into the living room like I was a thief in the night, cursing under my breath because I really should have taken the spellbook and my wand into the bedroom to keep them safe. What if they got stolen? Aunty Clem wouldn't be a happy bunny, or she might turn me into one! Could she? I shook my head at the notion. I was definitely letting my imagination run wild.

But I needn't have worried, as it seemed at least somebody had the sense to look out for things. Curled up fast asleep on the box was Harlow, his cute nose and whiskers twitching as he dreamed. I wondered what his dream would be about. Most likely nuts.

"Harlow, can I open the box, please?" I said softly, not wanting to shock him.

Our new friend opened an eye and grumbled about being disturbed, then yawned—who knew squirrels yawned?—before stretching out much like a cat does. He bared his teeth in what I took to be a smile, and I smiled back at him.

With his red fur bristling and fluffy after shaking himself out, he was seemingly satisfied so hopped onto my shoulder and nuzzled my ear in a way I was beginning to enjoy. The bizarreness of the situation wasn't lost on me, but I liked it and I liked him, so I told him so. He chattered away to me, and it was like he was saying he liked me too. Was this my imagination, or had something happened to him when all those magical items and powders, potions, and whatnot had assaulted him in the tree? It must have done something as he was incredibly smart and understood what people were saying, and I was pretty sure that was not normal for squirrels, even rare red ones.

"Thank you for guarding the book and wand. I know it was lax of me, and I won't forget again."

Harlow nibbled my ear gently, then jumped down and called for me to follow. I picked up the book and wand, then headed into the kitchen where he was already waiting by the door to the garden.

"Need a pee, eh?" I chuckled, then unlocked the door and let him out.

After making a morning coffee—the caffeine was always welcome—I stepped out into what promised to be another glorious day. I left the book and wand on the cast iron table on the patio, then sipped my coffee as I sauntered across the garden, then stopped abruptly as Harlow began to make a right racket. What had got into him? He was going crazy making a high-pitched scream as though he was injured. I put my mug on the table and raced across the lawn past several curved flower beds and over to the right where the deep border was already shimmering with life.

"Where are you, Harlow? What's going on?" I whispered, not wanting to wake the neighbours, then dodged the shrubs as someone screamed, "Ow! Get off me, you filthy creature."

A head popped up and I was amazed to find Frank batting at Harlow as the guard squirrel scratched and bit at his face. Luckily, he had his felt cap on or it would have been much worse, but his nose was bleeding and he had a nasty claw mark on his cheek. Frank grabbed Harlow by the neck and I was sure he was about to ring his neck before I hissed, "You better not dare hurt him or I'll do much worse to you."

Harlow looked at me with pleading eyes as Frank turned and spied me for the first time. The vicious grin of a man about to enjoy hurting an innocent creature immediately faded, quickly replaced with a friendly smile. But he couldn't hide his true nature from me, and I was probably more surprised to discover the kind of man he was than Frank was to find me out in the garden at this time.

More to the point, what was he doing here?

"Oh, hello, Lucas. Gosh, you gave me a start there. Bit early for you to be up, isn't it?"

"I could say the same about you. At least I'm where I'm supposed to be. Which I absolutely cannot say about you. Get out of the bushes, Frank. You're ruining Clem's hard work. Look at it."

Frank stared at the broken stems of several prized hibiscus in full, glorious purple bloom and winced. "Oops. Sorry about that, but this cute little fellow gave me a scare. He attacked me! Can you believe it?"

Harlow hissed at Frank then made a break for freedom and darted through the undergrowth, then climbed up the fence and sat atop it, letting loose with a tirade of abuse aimed at Frank before turning to me and continuing his complaining.

I waited impatiently while Frank stepped cautiously from the border, but tried not to act like I'd seen what he was about to do. More would be learned if I kept this light, and let him try to explain his actions, but I was also mindful of his every move, and ready to deal with him if he tried anything. He was clearly taking a big risk coming here and was obviously capable of violence.

"What are you doing here, Frank? You're trespassing, and you're upsetting Harlow."

"That creature... that squirrel? It has a name?"

"Yes, and it doesn't like people sneaking around. Neither do I? Why are you here?"

"Well, it's the funniest thing," he said, removing his flat cap and scratching his silver hair. "I couldn't sleep thinking about poor Clem, and what you'd said, and then it came to me. There might be clues, something you or the police overlooked. I've spent a lot of time out here over the years, so thought maybe I could uncover something nobody else had. And, er, that's what I was doing."

"You didn't think to ask first? You just came here without permission and snooped around?"

"I didn't think you'd mind. I know Clem won't. And I didn't know you were even here. Sorry to cause you any bother. I guess I'll be going." Frank hitched up his jeans and I noticed red string wrapped around his belt in place of the keeper.

"What happened to your belt?" I asked, keeping my tone friendly.

Frank looked down and his lip curled before the tic vanished and he smiled warmly as he said, "Oh, this? The keeper broke and while I was out there looking I found a piece of string by the trees. Figured it would do the job perfectly, and it does."

"Okay," I said, face neutral.

"Look, I'm sorry about this, and I didn't find anything anyway. But I just wanted to help out. I can't bear to think of someone trying to harm my good friend, not to mention there being a murderer on the loose. I guess this does appear rather suspicious, but I was just trying to help."

"That's fine, Frank, no problem. And sorry to be so rude. You just startled me, and I'm on edge after what's happened."

Frank nodded, then strode off, but I called after him, "Frank, that thing yesterday with the keys. You're a magic user, aren't you? Do you call yourself a wizard?"

"A wizard? No, just a mechanic with a touch of the gift. But I'm not like the others. I don't belong to a coven or anything. I just fix cars." With a nod, he left via the side path.

As if waiting for him to depart, Charlie came down the garden bearing two cups of coffee. She turned to watch Frank leave, then gave me an inquisitive look. She took in my sour mood and asked, "Something up? What was he doing here so early? Problem with the van?"

"No, not the van, but there's a problem with him. He's always been so nice, a family friend as long as I can remember, but I just saw the other side of our jovial mechanic. If I hadn't spotted him, he would have strangled Harlow."

"What? The poor thing. Harlow, are you okay?" she called to the watchful squirrel on the fence.

Harlow nodded, then jumped to a tree before racing over and nuzzling her neck nervously. Charlie handed me a mug and used her free hand to smooth his fur as the shaking creature slowly relaxed.

"Um, thanks. But now I have two."

Charlie smiled at the sight of me holding two mugs and said, "Then drink up before they get cold."

"Frank got caught snooping by Harlow, then grabbed him and was trying to throttle the poor guy. I saw the evil look on his face. And then he made some excuse about not being able to sleep, and wanting to search for clues."

"At this time of the morning? Not very likely."

"And that's not all. He had the red string around his belt to use as a keeper. Said he found it here. I think it might be him."

"But it's Frank. Sweet old man who works his magic on the vehicles. Excuse the pun. Maybe he did find the string."

"Maybe. Anything's possible. But you should have seen his face. It was really nasty. I've encountered that look before, more times than I can recall, and it's the sure sign of a bad person. Someone spiteful, nasty, rotten to the core. He's been hiding behind this friendly persona, when in reality he'd strangle a sweet squirrel and enjoy it."

"How did he have Harlow?"

"Harlow was attacking him."

"Lucas, then he was defending himself. You're reading too much into this. If Harlow attacked him, what else could he do?"

"Not enjoy killing him." I stroked Harlow's fur and he lifted his head so I rubbed under his chin then his ear as he leaned into it just like a dog would. "You were just guarding us, weren't you?"

Harlow nodded. Seemingly calm now, he left us to go do whatever squirrels did early in the morning.

"Are you sure about this?" asked Charlie, watching me closely. "You aren't reading more into it than you should?"

"Absolutely not. He looked vicious. And the fact he was here at all is beyond weird. Who comes snooping at the crack of dawn? Oh, sorry, love. Good morning. Couldn't sleep?" I pecked her on the cheek and tried to relax, smiling at the love of my life.

"Nope. I woke up and you weren't there, so couldn't get back to sleep. I figured I might as well get an early start."

"Sorry I disturbed you."

"You didn't. And even if you had I would understand. You're worried about Clem. We all are. Hopefully, she'll be home today. So, what's the plan?" Charlie smiled, eyes twinkling, then sipped at her coffee.

"The plan is to go and visit Shirley, and possibly Em, as then we will have spoken to everyone who was here. But so far, it isn't looking like it was any of them. Do you think it could be Frank? How could he have done it?"

"You said yourself that he knows magic. If that's true, and I'm not doubting your word, then it could be any number of ways, couldn't it? We need to speak to Clem and figure out just how powerful they all are. Is this just little pieces of magic, or can they do serious harm with it?"

"Someone did. By killing Sylvester. I wonder if he had any enemies. Maybe we should speak to his family."

"No, that's a very bad idea. We already decided not to. They don't know us, and they'll be grieving. He only passed yesterday. It's too soon. And besides, the police will have spoken to them. Let's wait until Clem is home and see what she thinks. Maybe she knows them. That would be a better solution."

"You're right. I'm not thinking clearly. But things just don't add up and I still can't understand why this was dismissed so quickly by the police. Maybe DI Durham did it. That would make total sense. He could cover it up, plant evidence, and just bury this whole thing as an accident. Which, I might add, is exactly what's happened."

"Stop it." Charlie shook her head and sighed. "You're just being silly now. Why would he murder Sylvester? Why do it in such a strange way? Why trip Clem and blow up the attic? No, you're getting carried away. Stick to the facts and we'll figure this out. I'll come with you to speak to Shirley, but let's face it, there's no way it was her. She's what, seventy? And frail as a..." Charlie frowned and asked, "What's frail?"

"I think the saying is frail as a kitten, but now I've said it that doesn't sound right."

"It's weak as a kitten."

"You're right. Ah, I remember. It's frail as a dragonfly's wings, but, um, where were we?" I asked, losing my train of thought.

"Just drink your coffees, you daft man. And stop suspecting everyone. Next you'll be saying it could have been Young Dave."

"He did turn up just after it happened. A bit convenient, don't you think?"

"Lucas!" Charlie giggled as she punched me playfully on the arm. "I think we can both guarantee Young Dave is not going around murdering accountants."

"Or is he?" I asked, eyebrows raised, but unable to stifle a chuckle.

"No, he isn't. You're so silly."

"I'm just going to check in the bushes, make sure he hasn't planted anything."

"You're getting obsessed. What would he do that for? Nobody's coming back to look again."

"I don't know, but I need to do it anyway."

With Charlie waiting, I pushed apart the tall shrubs, tried to avoid stepping on anything, and eased into the dense, high planting. This was a cottage style planting border, with a wild array of colours and textures, everything jumbled together but working in complete harmony somehow. The plants at the rear up against the neighbouring fence were almost as high as the fence itself, rich dark elder and joyous perpetual sunflowers even higher.

I checked everywhere I could, but found nothing, advancing right up to the fence. There was a weird smell, but as far as I could tell it was merely the fencing itself, installed only last year in the winter to replace the old, rotting panels. Most had already seasoned, going a nice silver colour, but one section was still looking rather fresh, most likely because it was where the densest planting was. Although, it was looking rather patchy in places where the plants had snapped. That idiot Frank had probably done it, but I couldn't find any broken pieces. Hardly surprising when I was in what amounted to a jungle.

With nothing to show for my search but damage to delicate shrubbery, I emerged as carefully as I could to find Charlie waiting with the coffees at her feet and Harlow back in her arms.

We walked back up the garden, then sat on the hard, weather-worn chairs and I eyed the book and wand suspiciously while I drank my coffees.

"What are you thinking?" asked Charlie.

"If this is some weird joke I don't understand, and there's no such thing as magic. I still can't come to terms with it. I mean, seriously?"

"I think that deep down you've always known it's true. That there must have been signs. What about your mum? Did she ever show you anything magical?"

"No, and she wasn't happy when Clem began what she called "foolish nonsense." Mum's not into anything she could label "hippy stuff" or "airy fairy." Come to think of it, her and Clem had a bit of a falling out when all this began. They still aren't like they used to be even now. Not that Mum's around as much now she's got that place in Spain. She was upset to hear about her though, but it isn't like she's come rushing around to check on things. That's sisters for you, I guess."

"Maybe it's a ruse? But they seem friendly enough now. Your mum's always popping in when she's home. And Clem visits her."

"Yes, but they were much closer. Maybe it's just their age. Mum should be here."

"So, go on then." Charlie nodded at the book and wand, and I gulped. "Are you nervous?"

"Yes," I admitted. "But what if this is a trick? Someone's idea of a game? There might be something in the wand to make it sparkle and the rest was just my imagination."

"You cleaned Young Dave's brush. And what about Miranda? We both saw that. She conjured images from the past. That was no joke. It was real."

"I know, but still."

With an encouraging nod from Charlie, I picked up the wand and wondered why I'd been so hesitant. It was warm, and somehow it just felt right. Like a part of me that had been missing my entire life. Like I was finally complete.

I paged through the book awkwardly, fingers trembling, and laughed at my own nerves. What had got into me? I paused when I found a likely candidate and showed it to Charlie whose eyes went wide.

"You think?" she gasped, then beamed at me with building excitement.

"Why not? It's worth a shot. Are you sure about this? I get the feeling that once this starts, there's no stopping it. Do you want a wizard as a husband?"

"You're already magical to me. You make my life full of wonder. Of course I'm sure."

"You're way too good for me. I'm a painter, and we aren't exactly swimming in money."

"You make a good wage, and so do I. We do alright for ourselves. And money doesn't bring happiness. You do."

With a smile, I read over the spell again. Either this would work, or I was going to feel like an utter fool.

Chapter 13

I stood, gripping the wand tight, and felt the power inside it—or was it inside me?—grow. I read the words on the open page again, just to get a feel for them, then spoke the spell out loud.

"To save the fuss, fill up the cups," I said, trying to get the words to flow smoothly like a gentle summer rain. I knew there was a rhythm, and felt that I'd got it right, something clicking in my mind and a connection made that felt different to the other times. With a practised swish, I tapped the edge of both our empty cups and a spark flashed from the wand then circled the rims.

As we watched, so both cups began to fill, and fill, and fill until they overflowed for a moment until the afterglow of the spell vanished, leaving two steaming drinks that certainly smelled like coffee.

"You're a real wizard!" gasped Charlie, cheeks flushed.

"I wouldn't go that far, but there's certainly no denying this is real. Want to go first?" I indicated the drinks, but she shook her head.

"No way. What if it's gross? You do it."

Tentatively, I lifted the cup, sniffed, and then sighed. "Smells amazing." I sipped cautiously, then whooped. "It tastes even better."

We both drank eagerly, delighting in the bitter tang of probably the best coffee I had ever tasted.

"Does this mean we can chuck out the kettle and save on the shopping bills?" asked Charlie, only half joking.

"I honestly don't know. How does this work? Where does it come from? I mean, the water, milk, and coffee have to come from somewhere, right? Are we stealing someone else's morning cuppa? Is there some poor soul staring in amazement at their empty cup while we drink it?"

"Clem will know. We'll ask her later. I'm very proud of you, Lucas Moran. You should have seen the way you acted. You looked like you knew what you were doing. Very wizardly. Just don't go getting a pointy hat and a cape."

"I won't," I laughed, beyond relieved that this had worked. Concerned that it had, too. All of a sudden, I was aware that I had a very different future to the one I'd expected to have. Life would never be the same again for either of us. I knew it, and it scared me.

As if reading my mind, Charlie said, "Think of it as a good thing. Sure, it's a surprise, but it's a wonderful one. How amazing to know there truly is real magic in the world? And anyway, you only have to do it if you want to."

"True. But what if I can't resist?" Suddenly, I felt exhausted, and slumped into the chair. "Ah, yes, I forgot about the side-effects. Guess that answers my own question. No way could you do this much in a day. You'd be too tired to even lift the wand."

"So finish your drink, rest up, and I'll make us breakfast. Young Dave will be down the moment he smells bacon frying."

"Now that's true magic. He can smell a rasher from a mile away," I chuckled.

Charlie left, so I sank back into the chair, sipping the magical coffee with equal amounts of suspicion and awe. What was the First Law of Thermodynamics? That energy can be converted from one form to another, but it can never, ever be created. So how did this thing called magic work? Where did the energy come from? What about the coffee? Was it even real coffee or a spell of some kind to make us believe we were drinking it?

I took another sip, It sure tasted real. It was wet, hot, strong, and yes, authentic. Aunty would know, right? I wondered if Mum did know about any of this, and that was why she was so adamant it was just crazy nonsense and refused to even talk about it. Was that why she ran off to Spain? Come to think of it, didn't she leave just a few months after Clem took up her hobby? Now she spent her time hanging out with ex-pats by the beach, and when she did come home she looked like a walnut wearing inappropriate clothes even in the winter. Mum would constantly complain about how cold it was, yet refused to wear jumpers as she just found them too constricting after spending so much time in vests and shorts in Marbella. Still, it was nice to have somewhere to go and have a cheap holiday, but I'd have liked her to have been around more to get to know Charlie better. Plus, I did miss her.

"Cooee!" came a familiar voice, and my heart both sank and leaped at the same time. I hurriedly grabbed the spellbook and wand, put them in the box, and searched for a place to hide it, not wanting to get into an argument immediately. I stashed the box behind a plant pot and turned, genuinely pleased, but also surprised, to see my mother standing there in all her suntanned glory. Mum's thin frame was burned dark by the Spanish sun, her dyed blond hair long and straight, intense brown eyes all the more penetrating for the tan. She wore a yellow vest and a pair of white shorts, with leather sandals, and she beamed at me as she held out her arms for a hug.

"Mum, what are you doing here? Is everything okay?" I wrapped my arms around her, taking in the familiar smell of Oil of Olay, her usual perfume, and just the essence of Mum.

"Everything's fine." Mum kissed me on the cheek, then we broke apart and she asked, "What's been going on? I called the hospital and they said Clem's doing well, but is she really? What happened?"

"I told you on the phone what happened. Nothing's changed. She had an, er, accident on the stairs, the attic blew up, and someone died in the garden."

"Yes, and that sounds awful, but I want the truth. I've been up all night trying to get back here, and I don't want you trying to fob me off with some nonsense about her tripping. Clem has used those stairs thousands of times and never tripped. My sister does not trip. I know her, and I know you, and you're keeping secrets. Both of you."

"It's a long story," I sighed, "and you won't like it. I can't believe you came back so fast. How did you do it?"

"I got a taxi to the airport, booked a flight, then got a taxi here. Cost an absolute fortune. I can't believe they're allowed to charge such ridiculous prices."

"You should have called. I could have picked you up."

"Nonsense." She waved away the notion. "I'm not rattling around in that smelly van. It's combustible. You shouldn't have flammable things in a vehicle."

"I'm a painter and handyman. If I don't have combustibles, I won't have a job. I could have used Charlie's car."

"No, it was fine. It was the middle of the night anyway. Seems like I arrived just in time, though. Charlie said she'll do me a fry-up. Can't get the right bacon in Marbella. It's this weird Spanish stuff." Mum wrinkled her nose like it was done on purpose just to annoy Brits, same as so many ex-pats did when they talked about British staples they simply didn't have on the continent.

"Imagine that," I chuckled.

"Sorry, I'm being silly. You know I like it there, and I adore the people. But now and then you want a proper taste of home. And to see your boy and his darling wife," gushed Mum, smiling warmly as Charlie came out into the garden.

"How are you both holding up?" Mum took Charlie's hands and squeezed them affectionately, then smiled at her. She'd always loved Charlie from the first time they met back when we were dating, and Charlie liked her too. Mum was funny, warm, kind, and always loving, which had made it doubly strange when she and Clem fell out for a while.

"We're doing good, Bee. It's been a strange time, but there's lots to tell you and we've been trying to figure things out."

"Tell me all about it. But can we eat first? I'm ravenous. I could eat a Spanish donkey, tail and all." Mum laughed, the crow's feet at her eyes more prominent than ever.

"Sure. It'll only be a few minutes," said Charlie. "I still can't believe you're here. It must have been a long night."

"The longest. But I'm here now, and that's the main thing. Poor Clem. Imagine this going on in your own house. And before either of you start," Mum released Charlie and stood back to get a proper look at us, "I am not going to say I told you so when I see her. But I think we know exactly what's been going on here, don't we?" Mum put her hands on her hips and glared at us.

"Um, what?" I asked, nonplussed.

"It's her creepy friends, isn't it? All that woo-woo silliness about spells and magic and crystals. They've been meddling in things they shouldn't have and this is what you get. But where's the crime scene tape? Where's the police presence? Have they solved it already? Is Clem safe now from the assassin?"

"I don't think we need to be talking about assassins. But no, they haven't solved it. Or, they have, but not how they should have. It's complicated. Let's eat, then we'll tell you all about it."

"I knew this would lead to trouble," Mum muttered. "Be back in a mo," she added, then headed inside, most likely to use the bathroom.

Charlie and I had a quick chat while we sorted out breakfast, and right on cue Young Dave appeared looking like he'd been dragged through a hedge backwards. He yawned as he scratched at his unmentionables through a pair of designer ripped jeans, his scrawny upper body devoid of clothes.

"Do I have to stare at your ribs while I eat my sausage?" I grumbled.

"Depends if you want to or not. Yum, I smell a fry-up," he beamed, winking at Charlie.

"Sit yourself down and let's eat," said Charlie as she laid out four plates of eggs, sausage, hash browns, bacon, baked beans, and a plate loaded so high with toast it threatened to get butter on the ceiling.

"Four?" asked Young Dave. "Do I get to have two? Or is one for Harlow?"

"This would probably kill Harlow," I said, eyeing it greedily.

"And most likely us. We had sausages yesterday."

"We're stressed. We need this to get us going. It's going to be a long day," mumbled Young Dave, already ripping a slice of toast in half greedily.

"Mum's here. She just arrived," I told him, then got to work.

"Cool. I like Bee."

"Did somebody mention my name?" asked Mum, beaming at Young Dave as she came in and almost drooled as she spied breakfast. "Oh my! Thank you so much, Charlie. This is just what the doctor ordered. Can't wait." Without preamble, she sat down and began to eat.

We chatted over breakfast, telling Mum what had happened but without too much detail and no mention of magic, which made it rather awkward to explain everything, but I didn't want to get into it with Young Dave here. He knew how she felt about it, as I'd told him before he first met Mum, but she was no fool and it was clear we were withholding things from her.

Mum asked repeatedly about Clem, truly concerned, and lamented that they weren't as close as they had been. I didn't push it, but this had genuinely shocked her, and maybe it was a wake-up call for them both.

It wasn't long before everyone was setting their cutlery down, and in her usual no-nonsense manner, Mum said, "You know I'm not an idiot, so tell me what's really been going on." She crossed her arms and gave us each the Mum stare; we squirmed in our seats.

Young Dave was the first to break, being the youngest, and blurted, "Lucas can do magic. And we have a magical squirrel named Harlow. Someone booby-trapped Clem, and we think maybe the police planted evidence."

"No we do not!" I hissed.

"And we found clues and are investigating. We're going to visit one of the coven this morning before Clem gets home, and wow, magic is real. Can you believe it?"

"I think you better start again, but slowly," said Mum, glaring at me but patting Young Dave on the knee. "You're a good lad, but you should learn to keep secrets."

"But you wanted to know. And you were glaring. How can I keep quiet when you stare at me like that?" He inspected his already clean plate, too timid to risk another laser glare.

Mum laughed, then without anger asked me, "What's this about a cover-up? We'll get to the magic later."

I explained about how quickly the police had inspected the scene and taken the body away, and that they'd found nothing, but then we'd found the crystal ball and they'd basically shut the case down, saying it was an accident. Forensics had confirmed this and the whole thing was basically dismissed as an unfortunate accident. Mum remained silent throughout, then mulled it over for a while after I'd finished.

"That makes perfect sense."

"It does?" asked Charlie.

"Yes. Clem's husband was a very important man in the police force. He knew everyone and everyone liked him. There are still quite a few of them working, top brass kind of people who don't take no for an answer. They wouldn't want Clem being hounded by the press, or have her getting more upset than necessary, so would have made this a priority. No police hanging around, no crime scene tape if possible, and when they want things done it gets sorted pronto. I know it seems strange to you, but this isn't exactly a place brimming with serious crime. When the bigwigs want things done, they get done."

"But still, that's not how they do things on the TV or in crime books. There are always delays and red tape."

"That's not real life. In the real world, things either drag on forever or people actually do their jobs properly and find out the truth. The forensics team and the police did their jobs. If the attic blew up, then it stands to reason that's what killed that man, Sylvester. It was lax that they didn't find the crystal ball immediately, but they all had their bosses breathing down their necks. But don't forget, Clem's husband was an important man and nobody would want his name sullied. Certainly not with the suspicion of a murder at his home. They did it for him and for Clem."

"So you think it was an accident?"

"Of course not! I already told you. It's very unlikely Clem tripped. And whoever's heard of somebody getting killed by a crystal ball punching right through them?"

"But it had his DNA on it," said Young Dave.

"Maybe it did. Doesn't mean it somehow miraculously flew over the roof then shot through him. What else?" asked Mum, now totally in no-nonsense mode.

"We found a nail and a piece of string on the stairs where Clem tripped. Someone did it on purpose."

"Show me."

We dutifully did, and Mum inspected it closely before standing and confirming, "No way would she have overlooked that in the past. She loves these stairs."

"That's what I told DI Durham, but he dismissed it."

"Because it's much easier to believe she tripped than someone set her up. What next?"

We explained about finding the string outside, then the explosion and Harlow, and him finding the crystal ball. And then I told her about Frank and how he was snooping around this morning.

"I never liked that man. You could tell he had a nasty streak."

"You could? I thought you liked him. Why did you always use him?"

"Because your father, God rest his soul, thought very highly of him and they went way back. Friends a long time. He never saw it, but I could tell. He's got shifty eyes."

"You say that about everyone," I laughed.

"Only the shifty ones."

"And he had some of the red string on his belt. He might have done this, and planted the crystal ball, and he was back checking he hadn't left anything behind. Or maybe he lost the string and was looking for it."

"Could be. And now, why don't we go outside and get the most important thing out of the way?"

"What do you mean?" I asked, knowing exactly what she meant.

"Don't take me for a fool, Lucas Moran. Magic. That's what. Come on. All of you."

"Do I have to come?" asked Young Dave nervously.

"Yes, you do," said Mum. "And then you can do the dishes."

"Aw, not fair."

We dutifully trailed behind the powerhouse known as Bee, Queen Bee more like. Mum took control of situations, whether anyone else wanted her to or not.

Chapter 14

"Out with it then. And don't think I didn't see you hide that box behind the plant pot."

I shook my head and laughed. "There's no hiding anything from you, is there?"

"Of course not, dear. I'm your mother. I always know. So don't do anything wrong."

Pushing down the rising panic at being confronted by such an all-powerful being, most likely from another dimension, I said, "So, what do you want me to tell you?"

"Everything. It's magic, isn't it? That's behind all of this. Clem and her silly coven. All this playing with dangerous forces. She should know better. She does know better. Now look what's happened. She could have been killed."

"I thought you didn't believe in any of it?"

"Maybe I do, maybe I don't. That's not the point."

"Of course it's the point. Do you believe in magic?"

"Depends on your definition," said Mum evasively, as she suddenly found the garden interesting. "Ooh, lovely acers. Aren't they just a joy? So exotic."

"Mum, stick to the point. Why did you and Clem fall out? The real reason?"

Mum took a seat and became serious. "I told her not to get involved in this. I knew it would lead to trouble."

"What do you mean, Bee?" asked Charlie.

"Are you a witch like Clem?" asked Young Dave, eyes wide as he took a step back.

"No, and don't you dare call me that!" Mum hissed, then her face softened and she said, "Sorry, didn't mean to snap. But it's a sore point."

"What is?" I asked, amazed this was the first I was hearing about any of whatever this was.

"We have magic in our bones, son." Mum's shoulders sank, and yet she held her head high and locked her eyes on mine. "I'm sorry to tell you, but it's in your blood. From my side of the family. It goes back a long way, and it's been nothing but trouble. When Clem and I were young, my big sister, and remember there's quite an age gap, and I pestered our mother non-stop to show us and teach us what she knew. It went horribly wrong and Clem and I promised never to go near the nasty stuff again."

"You never said. Why not?"

"Because I didn't know if you had it inside, and there was no way I was going to ask you. Magic isn't for the likes of us, and it never does you any good. It leads to nothing but disaster. And I was right. Now it has."

"So what happened?"

"I don't want to talk about it. We made a pact, and Clem broke it. We went through all these years not daring to even pick up a crystal, we didn't even have playing cards just in case our gifts tried to emerge, and she went and ruined everything by getting involved with these fools who most likely don't have a magical bone in their bodies."

"They do. At least some do. Miranda conjured an image of Clem falling down the stairs."

"Did she now? That's interesting. Quite advanced. But you can't trust it. Things like that aren't to be relied upon. You can just as easily see what you want to see, rather than the truth. I'm warning you, it's not worth the risk involved."

"But Lucas cleaned my brushes. What's the harm in that?" asked Young Dave.

"What will be next? Using magic to clean the house? Then you'll be left exhausted, maybe even paralysed if you push things too far. And besides, if you tried to use magic to do everything, what would be the point of you being around? There are some things best left alone, and magic is definitely one of them."

"But you won't say what happened to you both?" I asked as I sat beside her and held her hands. "It's okay, you can tell us."

"No, never. Please don't ask again. But don't meddle in things you don't understand. Any of you."

"Can anyone do it?" asked Young Dave eagerly.

"Afraid not. You have to have the gift, something inside you. It's very rare, and most wouldn't even know if they had the power. How would you? Although, some people can see ghosts, or get glimpses of the future, and that's just a miserable life. Ugh." Mum shuddered at the thought. I had to agree. That would not be fun.

"So what you said about Aunty Clem being silly and you calling it hippy nonsense was just a ruse to put me off?"

"I didn't want to tell you the truth, now did I? And anyway, you wouldn't have believed me."

"I guess not. Unless you'd shown me."

"There you go then. What else could I do? Clem made a promise, and she broke it. Now she's got involved with these horrible people and look what happened. What a mess. Have you seen any of them? Spoken to them?"

We explained what we'd been up to, and that we were going to visit the elderly Shirley later on, and we still hadn't spoken to Em, the young girl.

"Guess I better come with you," sighed Mum.

"No way. You're exhausted, and we can't all go barging in there. She'll clam up faster than a... um... clam."

"Maybe you're right. Young Dave will keep me company, won't you?"

Young Dave looked at me, his eyes pleading, but I shrugged and said, "You're on your own with this one, buddy."

"Fine, I'll stay. But I want a full report when you get back. And in the meantime, Bee can tell all she knows about magic. Hey, think I've got it in me? Could I be a wizard like Lucas?"

"I am not a wizard. I just did a couple of spells."

"That's impressive," said Mum. "Normally, it takes months of practice to do even the easiest ones. If you ever can. It takes focus, strong nerves, and plenty of food and rest to recover. But how did you channel it? You don't have a wand."

"Actually, I do," I admitted, then retrieved the wand and book to show her.

"My, that's fine work." She admired the simple wand, then placed it gently on the book. "Did you make it?"

"No. We found it in the attic. Clem made it for me. She said she'd tell us more when she came home. Why did she make it for me, Mum? Why would she think I'd want it? And that goes against your agreement, I assume?"

"It does." Mum had a face like thunder, and yet I could tell she wasn't as angry as she was pretending to be.

"Come on, tell the truth."

"Fine," she sighed. "We agreed never to even think about a spell, let alone use proper magic, unless it was an emergency. And I'm guessing that whatever happened here counts as one."

"But she didn't make it yesterday. Are you saying she knew this was coming?"

"All I'm saying is that both your aunty and I are gifted. Understand? We have the gift. She might be a little prescient. Me too. She probably made it just in case you'd need it. This is just terrible. I don't want you getting mixed up in this nonsense."

"Bit late for that. We're up to our necks in it. Can you tell me more? When I did the spells, I was exhausted, and couldn't do it the second time straight away. I had a go this morning and filled up our coffee cups, which was cool, but it has me worried."

"First Law of Thermodynamics?"

"Yes. How did you know?"

"Because we all have the same questions. How? Why? Where?" She waved it all away. "It's bloody magic. That's everything you need to know. Dangerous, with forces not to be messed with. And now here's Clem with a daft coven and a right bunch of clowns waving their wands around and getting themselves killed. So stupid."

"It's kept her spirits up for years. She's got a new lease on life, and friends. Something to do, people to talk with about what she enjoys. What's wrong with that?"

"Someone died, that's what. And it isn't the first time."

"How do you mean?"

"Nothing. And I think I need a lie down. I'm exhausted. When's Clem getting home?"

"Some time this afternoon, most likely. We have to wait to hear from the hospital."

"I'll give them a call in a few hours to check. But I need to rest. It's great to see you all, and Young Dave?"

"Yeah?"

"You doing okay?" Mum knew about his home life, and had a soft spot for him.

"Great, thanks. Lucas and Charlie have been looking out for me. Although I haven't had a pay rise," he added brightly.

"I'll have a word," she said, winking.

I groaned, knowing she wouldn't rest until Young Dave got what he wanted. He did deserve it, so I'd sort him out this month and make his position permanent. His apprenticeship wasn't up for another year, but I'd already decided to just take him on full-time anyway. He was part of the family now, and we looked after our own.

Mum kissed us all then left to take a nap, and Young Dave reluctantly clattered about in the kitchen making a big show of washing up. Charlie and I now had the opportunity to go and visit Shirley, and I thought it best to head off relatively early to catch her before she possibly went out for the morning. Plus, I didn't want to have to help Young Dave do the dishes.

"Ready?" asked Charlie a quarter of an hour later once we'd got ourselves ready and given the house a quick once-over with the Hoover just in case Clem was released early.

"Just one thing." I dashed out into the garden and called for Harlow, who raced up the garden from the trees and stopped in front of me, head cocked.

"We're going to visit Shirley. One of the coven members. Do you want to come? Maybe see if you can find anything out? You've been a great help so far." Harlow chattered away, tail swishing like he could sweep the lawn, "Can you understand me?" More chattering. "Let's try again. One grunt for yes, three for no, just so I can be sure you really do understand." Harlow grunted once. "That's awesome! Okay, one more question then we can go. Did Frank, that man in the garden this morning, kill Sylvester?" One grunt. My heart raced. Then two more in quick succession. "You sure?" One grunt. "Okay then, little buddy. I don't know how you know, but let's go find us a killer. Actually, let's go through them all." I gave the names, and Harlow insisted it was none of them, but then I asked the all-important question. "Do you know who did it?" Three grunts. "That's a shame. But let's be honest, there's no way you could know who it was, is there? You were out the front when it happened, then unconscious. You're just guessing, aren't you?" One grunt.

I chuckled as my new best buddy raced up my leg and draped himself across my shoulder. "I like you, Harlow. Do you like me?" One grunt. "That's good enough for me. Right, let's be off."

We took the Mini, and decided to pop home first to collect a few things as we'd be spending at least a few days with Aunty Clem. It made sense as our house was on the way to Shirley's. I felt almost nervous going back to the home Charlie and I had shared for five years now. We moved in together three months after we met, and hadn't been apart since. It was my mortgage to begin with and it had been crippling me, but once we knew we were destined to be together, we'd changed it into joint names and opened a joint bank account. We didn't have separate money or accounts, just a shared one, and paid for everything out of that. Neither of us were big spenders; we trusted one another, and it had worked out perfectly ever since.

But I felt like a different person after just a day. As though everything was brand new. I guess it was. I certainly wasn't the same, and doubted I ever would be again. Just like when I left the armed forces, I realised that person was no longer who I was, although a part always remained. Now I was changing again. But none of it compared to when I finally realised I had a chance with Charlie. That was when I truly became a different man. Whole. Capable of loving and being loved. And finally accepting that I deserved to be happy. To be more than just coasting along keeping my head above water, but to truly enjoy life and be content. Charlie gave me that and so much more.

The moment we were through the door, all my concerns vanished. This was our home, our sanctuary. I breathed in the familiar smells, took in the stylish but simple furniture. The cushions on the sofa, the light shades, the rugs, and polished floors. Our detached Victorian home was a three-bedroom palace in comparison to how most people lived, and I'd got it for a bargain price because of the renovation work needed. It took me two years of non-stop toil and it was worth every minute. Now we had a gorgeous, spacious home with simple furnishings and it was ours.

"It feels like we've been gone for weeks," I groaned, slumping onto the sofa and breathing in deeply.

"I know, and I was here yesterday afternoon to grab some spare clothes and stuff for dinner. Too much has happened. How are you holding up? It was a shock to see Bee. She's such a character."

"She sure is. Can you believe that about magic? She knew, and always has. I wonder what happened when they were younger to set her against it like this? And I can't understand why she wouldn't tell me, especially once her sister started dabbling again."

"Because she didn't want you to get into it. I'm sure she has her reasons. And besides, it's all out in the open now."

"Not all of it. But I'm sure it will be soon enough. At least she came back. That was really good of her."

"She's a kind woman. Tough, but kind. Let's grab our things and get going, because I don't know about you, but I could happily spend the day lazing on the sofa watching movies."

"Don't tempt me," I groaned. "Instead, we have to deal with Mum, Aunty Clem, go visit Shirley, and who knows what else."

Something scratched at the underside of the sofa, making us both shriek and jump up.

"An intruder!" screamed Charlie as she grabbed a lamp.

A little red head popped out from underneath and Harlow purred, almost like a cat. He climbed up and sat on the back rest, watching us intently.

Charlie laughed with nervous relief then replaced the lamp.

"Sorry for being so rude, Harlow. We didn't offer to invite you in. I forgot you were there because you fell asleep in the car. How do you like the place? It's our home," I explained.

Harlow purred again, and added a coo.

"You like it, don't you?" laughed Charlie. Harlow grunted once.

"That means yes," I told her. "We learned it this morning. One grunt for yes, three for no."

"Why not two?"

"Saves any confusion. Right?" I asked Harlow.

He grunted once.

"That's great! So, do you want the tour?"

Harlow grunted, then sprang onto Charlie's shoulder and they went to explore the house while I just wandered around checking on things like I hadn't been here just yesterday morning. I was feeling comfortable, if very tired. The spell with the coffee had drained me, and even a large fry-up hadn't restored me fully.

After inspecting the kitchen, I sank back onto the sofa and listened to Charlie talking to Harlow and him answering in a variety of squeaks, grunts, purrs, and several high-pitched sounds I hadn't heard before but to my ears sounded like contentment. Feeling the same, I closed my eyes just for a second.

"Time to go, sleepyhead," whispered Charlie as she shook my shoulder gently and smiled as I opened my eyes.

"Oh, sorry. Must have nodded off." I yawned, then stretched out, feeling better for the rest. "Was I out for long?"

"Just long enough for me to pack us some clothes and give Harlow the tour. Which is very convenient."

"You should have woken me. I would have helped."

"No, it's fine. All done. I think Harlow likes it here." Harlow sprang onto my lap and purred, the same sound he'd made earlier. "See. It's his happy sound. Like a cat."

"You want to move in with us?" I asked, joking. Harlow grunted. "What, really? I thought you lived in a tree?" Harlow shook his head, then raced to the living room door and began chattering away.

We followed after him and he went through the dining room then to the back door leading to the large garden. He jumped up onto the window sill by the table and chattered noisily.

"He's saying he wants to live out there, but with us," said Charlie.

"I think you're right. We do have a lot of trees bordering the property, and there are a few mature hazel trees. You want to do that, Harlow?" A definite grunt, backed up by a nod.

Charlie and I looked at each other, then shrugged. We turned to him and smiled.

"Welcome to the family, Harlow," I said, then laughed as he spun in a circle, fell off the sill, then raced over and scrambled up my leg and bounded onto my shoulder.

"Looks like we have a new member of the family," beamed Charlie.

"Sure looks that way. Right, let's get going. Harlow, we'll move back here in a few days once Clem is better. You good with that?" He grunted his answer, so it seemed like it was all settled.

Buoyed by this latest development, because we genuinely liked him, we headed off to visit Shirley and see what she could tell   us.

Chapter 15

"She lives here?" asked Charlie, slightly bemused by the rows of compact bungalows, the manicured lawns, and the sheer volume of elderly people either chatting in groups, sitting on the numerous benches, or strolling. Some with the assistance of walking sticks or Zimmer frames, whilst many were marching around proudly. Several sprightly octogenarians were even racing around the paths, wearing brightly coloured running gear, waving and smiling happily at everyone they passed.

"She's not as good on her feet as she used to be, apparently, so has been here for a few years. It's assisted living, but they each have their own little bungalow."

"Gran used to live in one, but it wasn't as fancy as this. She said the food they delivered was awful, and when you pulled the cord for one of the carers to come help you out, they took ages."

"I guess you get what you pay for. The few times I've met Shirley, she's always gushing about how they bring her incredible food whenever she wants and they have a gourmet chef. They have recreation evenings, there are activities in the afternoons, and the one time she had a fall and used the help button around her neck, they were there in a few minutes."

"Bet it costs a fortune."

"Probably. Look at the properties. They're very modern and swanky, have broad verandas, even private gardens at the back. You have to pay extra for a gardener, though."

"How does she afford it?"

"No idea. But she's a widower, so maybe she just sold her family home and this is what it gets you."

We took a moment to admire the clean estate, the lush trees, and the wildflower areas that contrasted nicely with freshly mown spaces for strolling or playing games, which several groups were. There were even a group of about ten doing Tai Chi, slowly moving from one position to another, all beaming happily as the young female instructor gave them the positions. Not surprisingly, there were more men than women.

"Harlow, you coming too?" I asked our miniature sleuth as he sat on the passenger seat waiting patiently.

With a grunt, he scampered out and raced across the grass to a tree then climbed up and sat on a branch to study the area.

"I think he's checking the coast is clear," laughed Charlie. "I don't think we have anything to worry about here, do you?"

"You never know. Some of these people look fitter than us."

"True. I really should take up running."

"Should, or will?" I asked, smiling knowingly.

"Should. But won't," she laughed.

With Harlow seemingly satisfied we weren't about to get attacked by a gang of pensioners beating us slowly over the head with walking sticks, Harlow came down the tree headfirst then kept between us as we made our way across the grass to find Shirley. I remember her saying that she lived in number 9 and it was fortuitous because that was her lucky number, but where that was became a mystery as we tried to figure out the numbering system of this well laid-out maze of homes.

After several minutes of fruitless searching, our presence was noted, and three women came over and began cooing over Harlow. A red squirrel was a rare sight, and to have one that was seemingly tame delighted the ladies. Their loud praise soon attracted the attention of others, and it wasn't long before we were surrounded by a sea of people clamouring for a chance to pet him. Harlow retreated to Charlie's shoulder, but that only served to intensify the attention, the comments on his fine fur, and requests to stroke him.

"Harlow, would you let the nice people stroke you very gently? Just a couple of strokes each? They think you're adorable and you are very rare." Harlow grunted once. "Harlow says yes," I told the group, and to be fair, they lined up like children at the beginning of playtime waiting to go out and let loose. With hardly contained excitement, one after another they each stepped forward and gently stroked his head or his back with often shaking, liver-spotted hands.

When everyone had their turn and we'd answered the numerous questions about how he was with us, Charlie had the foresight to ask after Shirley, stating we were friends of hers but couldn't find number 9. We were given the directions, and soon enough found ourselves at her bungalow.

"Do you think this is silly? There's no way she did it. She couldn't even pick up that crystal ball, let alone somehow..." I trailed off, not even knowing what to say.

"Ram it through Sylvester?"

"Yes, that."

"She might not have done it, but she might think of something that will help. And besides, who knows what powers she has. Now we know about them being a real coven, there's no saying what they might be capable of. Maybe she's been slighted by Sylvester and this was her revenge."

"You think?"

"No, I do not, but we need to speak to her anyway."

"You're enjoying this, aren't you?" I asked, knowing Charlie well enough to know when she was having a good time.

"A little," she admitted. "I know it was horrible what happened, but it is interesting, and it gets the brain ticking over trying to figure things out. We owe it to Clem, and we certainly owe it to Sylvester, to figure this out. Your aunt's life might be in danger."

"You're right. Let's tie her to a chair and shine a light in her eyes. That'll get Shirley to talk," I chuckled, then felt the colour drain from my face as Charlie nudged me insistently and I looked up to find Shirley staring at me, wide-eyed.

"Is that before or after I offer you tea and biscuits?" she asked, head cocked, her silver hair not budging thanks to the copious use of hairspray that was threatening to make me sneeze.

"After, of course," I laughed. "Can't do an interrogation before a cuppa."

Shirley chuckled, and said, "I assume you want to ask me about what happened? I'm surprised it took you so long." She stepped aside and gestured for us to come in, so we removed our shoes and entered.

The door closed behind us with a rather ominous thud, causing us to jump and Harlow to dash under the sofa to hide. We turned to find Shirley with her walking stick held high, but she smiled and lowered it.

"Sorry about that," I said. "I was only joking about the interrogation."

"I know that," she said sweetly, beaming at us. "No need to get heavy on me. I'll spill the beans." Shirley cackled, then mussed with her pink housecoat before slowly making her way over to a compact kitchen divided from the main living space by a gleaming counter.

"I'll put the kettle on. I don't get many visitors, so it's a treat to have company. Make yourselves comfortable. I won't be a moment. And is that a squirrel I see poking out from under my sofa? Is he the one from yesterday?"

"He is. That's Harlow. He's a victim of the explosion, and now he hangs out with us."

"That's good," she said, taking it in her stride.

Charlie and I exchanged a glance, then sat on the sofa. Harlow came and joined us, so we took a moment to check out Shirley's living arrangements.

The sofa was an old brown corduroy model I hadn't seen in decades, but it smelled fresh, was clean, and fit with the rest of the muted decor. Everything was brown, old, and polished to within an inch of its long life. The matching chair had a footrest and side table where Shirley clearly liked to sit. A bookshelf contained bits and pieces no doubt gathered over a lifetime, numerous Harlequin paperbacks, and a whole shelf of instruction manuals on crochet. The TV was older than me, a huge, bulbous thing cased in more brown veneer, sitting on a stand that looked ready to collapse at any moment. It was a typical elderly person's home, with furniture that was dated but functional, and comfortable in a way nothing modern ever was. A safe place, full of familiar things, with pictures of smiling faces on the walls and shelves, fake flowers in vases.

What took pride of place in this very mundane but comforting and cosy home was a modular Ladderax display unit of shelves and cupboards. No doubt owned since first introduced in the sixties, it was now a highly sort after and expensive retro piece of furniture with adjustable shelves and movable cupboards with sets of drawers spaced on several tiers. The shelves were laden with figurines of ballet dancers and even brass horse shoes and a ceramic Shire horse for good measure.

"Here's the tea," sang Shirley as she tried to manage a tray with a teapot, three cups, and a plate of biscuits whilst using her walking stick.

I jumped up and said, "Let me take that off your hands," then grabbed the tray before she dropped it.

"Thank you. I'm not as sprightly as I once was, but I still manage. Nice to have the old buzzer in case I need it though." Shirley fondled the lanyard around her neck with a bright red button that would call for help if she pressed it.

I placed the tray down on the table and Shirley sank gratefully into her chair then sighed as she put her feet up.

"How do you find it here?" asked Charlie.

"Lovely. Everyone's so sweet and kind and the gardens are a delight. We get to play bingo every day if we want to, there are bridge nights, even dances. And I'm going out of my mind."

Charlie paused midway to pouring the tea, and I almost choked on my biscuit.

"You don't like it?"

"Oh, it's fine." Shirley waved away any problems. "But they aren't really my crowd. So straight. They think taking a risk is going to bed after nine. There's no excitement. It's just going through the motions. Don't get me wrong, it suits most and they enjoy it, and I do too. But it's not my thing, you know?"

"What is your thing?" I asked, already knowing the answer.

"The coven. It's been my lifeline. My escape from drudgery. Something to really look forward to every week. We even get together other days sometimes to practice, or talk about what we've discovered. They're all such a great group, although I don't know the new girl very well yet. She seems nice though."

"We hadn't realised how important it was to you," I said.

"Not just me. All of us. People need an outlet, something to keep their minds active."

"True. Aunty Clem loves it. Shirley, is there anything you can tell us about what happened?"

"I can tell you I don't believe the police have it right. They were falling over themselves to save Clem from any embarrassment, and they were hardly going to believe that it was death by magical means, now were they?" Shirley leaned forward and studied us both closely to gauge our reactions, then smiled as she sank back into her chair. "Ah, I see you are believers. A lot can happen in a day, and I can see that you have changed your minds about our little coven."

"How can you tell?" asked Charlie.

"I see your aura. You're both good people, that goes without saying, but I see the way you shine, the way the magic is clinging to you both. Especially you, Lucas. You've been dabbling, haven't you?"

"I have. This is very new to us, and you know I never believed before, but yes, we do now. How long have you believed, Shirley?"

"All my life. Ever since I was a young girl I knew I was special. But you know how it goes. Life happens, you go to school, and it was different back in my time. I had a strict religious upbringing, and magic was not something to be discussed, let alone practised. Then I had a job for a while, got married, raised a family, and such things were forgotten. But when my dear husband died, and I found myself rattling around in my house all alone, the children all grown up and living their own lives, I began to look into it. And I found that I had the gift. Just like your aunt."

"And then you joined the coven?"

"Years later. I already knew what I was doing, so to speak, but the coven gives me direction, let's me talk about things openly, and it's nice to interact with people of different ages instead of just being with the wrinklies." Shirley laughed heartily, lines etched deep on her face, and added, "So, who do you think did it?"

"We have no idea," I admitted. "It could be anybody. Except you, of course."

"Oh, I could have done it easily enough. I'm powerful in my own way." Shirley lowered her head and stared at her legs propped on the stool, coy. "I'm not boasting, just telling it how it is."

"You mean your magic could have done that? And how about the others?"

"Maybe. I'm not sure about all of them, but I know Clem is strong, and Miranda is rather a force to be reckoned with. Mike's an odd one, and doesn't show anything to anyone, but I suspect he's probably more powerful than any of us. Of course, Sylvester was the best of us all, and liked to show off, but I guess he won't be doing that anymore."

"Guess not. You think Mike's got the skills to have done this?"

"Probably, but he's a sweet man under the tattoos and funny clothes. But he can be rather... How do I put this?"

"A bit dishonest?" suggested Charlie.

"Maybe. I never have quite trusted him, but I don't think it's anything malicious. He's just had a strange life and likes to keep things private."

"And now for the main question," I said. "Do you think it was magic that killed Sylvester?"

"What else could it have been?"

"We don't know. What happened in the garden?"

"Gosh, it was rather a blur. We were only out there a moment. I told the police what I could, but they weren't very interested in me. I get it all the time. They see a little old lady and think I'm harmless, but that's on them. Now, let me think." Shirley took a few moments to get her thoughts straight and have a drink of her tea, then said, "I believe I was talking with Sylvester, then I went to look at the flowers. Clem always has such a lovely garden. Then someone shouted, Mike, I think, and I turned and Sylvester was falling. He landed with a thud, and it was obvious he was dead."

"Could any of them have done that by, er, and wow, this sounds silly, blasting him with magic? Does it work that way?"

"That would be some very serious magic, so it's doubtful. We may be good, but creating a wound like that takes incredible force. If I did it, I'd be sleeping for a week. Magic use takes considerable energy unless you are extremely adept and been practising for many years. I can do regular spells without getting very tired, but something like that would have most people take to their bed for days."

"That's been a great help, Shirley. Thank you for your time."

"No problem at all. Now, excuse me, I must use the bathroom. You two finish your tea and don't let the biscuits go stale. I shan't be long."

Shirley stood with the aid of her stick, then disappeared down the hallway and closed the bathroom door. The moment she did, Harlow jumped from the sofa and ran over to the Ladderax unit and began clawing at a sliding door.

"Harlow," I hissed, "stop it. You'll scratch the wood."

Harlow turned to me then back to the door and scrabbled at it with his tiny, sharp claws.

"What's got into him?" said Charlie as we both stood.

"No idea. Is it a clue, Harlow?"

He grunted, then resumed attacking the defenceless cupboard. We moved either side of him, and with a shrug I slid the low door open.

Charlie and I jumped back in shock at what we discovered. Several crystal balls were lined up inside, with a thick book beside them. A wand lay atop the book, the wood almost black.

Glancing down the hallway, Charlie then opened another door to reveal a collection of books on magic, leather-bound, ancient tomes that looked rare and expensive, along with a collection of vials, and strange objects made from brass and steel.

"What is this stuff?" I whispered.

"Just her magic things."

Harlow chattered noisily so I shushed him, then we checked the rest of the cupboards, stealing glances back in case Shirley caught us. We found collections of hair in a box, tied in red string that I was beginning to realise they all seemed to use in one way or another. Maybe the coven had special magic string? We discovered several homemade effigies, simple dolls made of pieces of cloth with bits of material or hair pinned to them.

Charlie gasped as she opened the last cupboard then reached in to remove a large vial with layers of different powders inside.

"Those are the colours of the residue we found all over the front garden and on Harlow. What gives?"

"I don't know. Maybe they make the same potion with them. Or maybe not." Charlie frowned, then put it back as we heard the door open. We raced back over to the sofa and sat, then drank our tea, but we needn't have rushed as it took Shirley a while to join us.

"No need to see us out, but we have to go. Mum's in town for a visit to check on Clem, so we best be off. Thanks for the tea."

"Oh, are you sure? You won't stay for another cuppa?"

"Not today, thanks. Maybe another time? We appreciate your help, don't we, Charlie?"

"We do. Thank you. Bye."

Harlow dashed out of the door when Charlie opened it, and I had to force myself not to hurry, instead smiling at Shirley before I closed the door behind us once we'd got our shoes on.

Neither of us said a word as we trailed after an excitable Harlow back to the car, ignoring the cajoling pensioners clamouring to pet him. Once buckled up, Charlie sped off, and it wasn't until we were well away from the bungalow jamboree that either   of   us   spoke.

Chapter 16

"Is she a black magic witch?" I asked, not knowing the correct terminology but figuring I'd got it about right.

"I don't know. But why'd she have those effigies? Isn't that voodoo or something?"

"Possibly. And the hair. You saw that, right? With the string? Why does everyone have red string? Is it a witch and wizard thing?"

"Maybe. Or maybe they're all in on it, and ganged up on poor Sylvester."

"Shirley herself said she was a powerful magic user, and she had crystal balls. I can't think what else would have made the hole in Sylvester. Damn, they all have them, don't they?"

"Of course they do. It's part of their magic thing. But let's get real here." Charlie parked on a quiet side road and turned to me. "Just because a crystal ball was found in the bushes doesn't mean it's the one that killed Sylvester. The DI said Sylvester's blood was on the crystal ball, but maybe it wasn't that one at all. I just don't know. Maybe it did simply get overlooked."

"That's not very likely. They searched, so did we. It wasn't there. Someone put it there."

"But why? That's like going to the police station and handing in the murder weapon."

"Maybe they wanted us to find it."

"Again, why? It makes no sense. And besides, what's the point? And more to the point, how did they get it to go through poor Sylvester?"

"I don't know. Let's just get home. Shirley is one weird lady, but imagine if we didn't know how nice Clem is and went up into the attic. We'd assume she was the murderer."

"With those weird things in jars and the books on magic, then you're right. But she's the one person who we know is innocent. Right?" Charlie turned to me, eyebrows raised. "Right?"

"Yes. She fell, remember? And then they all went outside."

"Just checking. Gosh, I really am getting carried away with this. Maybe we're being silly and this is a mistake."

"Do you believe that?"

"No, but what are we supposed to do?"

"One last stop? See if we can have a chat with Em?"

"I doubt her father will let us. You heard what happened. He's a fancy lawyer. He's not going to let her talk to us."

"There's no reason not to," I said. "We aren't the police. We just want to have a quick word to see if she can help us out. He might be a nice guy."

"He's a lawyer."

"Hey, that's lawyerist!"

Reluctantly, Charlie agreed to drive over to her house. It didn't take long, and ten minutes later we found ourselves ogling what to all intents and purposes was a mansion. We stopped outside decorative wrought-iron gates with an intercom system on the wall, and simply sat, admiring a long, tree-lined gravel drive that led to an impressive home. I could picture a swimming pool, a games room, tennis courts, and all the other luxuries you expected swanky properties like this to have.

"You can probably fit a nine hole golf course in their living room," I noted as we peered at the wisteria-covered stone frontage.

"You don't know that. It looks big, but these places are often deceiving, with dingy rooms. Just lots of them."

"No way. I bet they have a swimming pool and a sauna. Go on then, press the buzzer."

Charlie pressed the intercom by reaching out of the window. A female voice asked, "Yes?"

Charlie explained who we were and asked if we could speak to Em, and that we just wanted to check she was alright and ask her a few questions as we were concerned for Clem's safety.

"No problem. Come right up. Park outside the house." The intercom buzzed then the gates swung open.

"Wasn't expecting that," I whistled.

"Neither was I. Let's go." Charlie wasted no time and drove through the gates up the gravel and into the shade of the trees before we emerged into bright light bouncing off the pale stone where she parked.

By the time we were out of the Mini, a woman was waiting on the steps, with Em beside her. Em had her head down as usual, and the woman seemed to be scolding her judging by the sour look on her face. But then she smiled at Em, gave her a cuddle, which Em reciprocated half-heartedly, and as we approached it was all smiles from the woman I assumed was her mother. Trim and athletic, wearing a tight tracksuit and running shoes with her raven hair in a ponytail and rather a lot of make-up, she greeted us warmly with a wave and a genuine smile.

"Hello. So lovely to meet some of Em's friends." She gave us the once over, then frowned and added, "Although you are much older than her. Em, are these your friends?"

"I thought I said," stammered Charlie. "We were at the house when the accident happened. At least my husband was. He's Clem's nephew."

"Yes, of course. I thought you were friends too?"

"Mum, I don't even know these guys," snapped Em.

"Oh, sorry. Well, I'm off for my Saturday run. You all be nice. And Em, I know this has been upsetting, but I'm sure these nice people just want to see if you know anything. After yesterday, and your father overreacting, I think that's the right thing to do. See you later." With a peck on her daughter's cheek, she was running down the drive.

"Guess you better come in," said Em, then turned and entered the house.

Harlow emerged from behind a large urn and followed us inside.

"Blimey," I blurted, taking in the scale of the interior. "This place is huge."

"Yeah, Mum and Dad love big houses. We've got seven bedrooms, three living rooms, even two kitchens if you can believe such a thing. I used to get lost going to the bathroom when I was a kid." Em turned and smiled at us, her hair parting to show a kind face. She favoured dark eye make-up and bright red lipstick, with faded ripped jeans and a Misfits tee, but her demeanour was friendly, if very sullen teen.

Harlow zig-zagged over to Em and sat at her feet, doe eyes staring up at her, his little arms outstretched.

"I think someone likes you," I laughed.

"Do you want a cuddle?" asked Em, smiling with delight.

Harlow coo-purred, then chattered excitedly, so Em reached down and scooped him up, her tense shoulders lowering.

"He's been with us ever since the explosion," I explained. "He seems to have become very smart, and he's helping us solve the case of the crystal ball conundrum.

"Huh?"

"I think we better explain. But first can we ask you some questions?"

"I guess. Let's go into the kitchen and I can make us a drink. Do you guys want coffee, or are you strictly tea drinkers?"

"A coffee sounds good. We just had tea at Shirley's."

"How is she? Shaken up, I bet. That's a lot for, um, someone of her age to deal with."

"Shirley seems fine. She's as tough as old boots, and, er—" I cast a glance at Charlie who just shrugged, so decided to tell Em what we'd found, "—we weren't snooping, but we found effigies. Little homemade dolls of people and bundles of hair tied with string in her cupboard. It freaked us out, actually, and we got out of there as fast as we could."

Em snorted in amusement, then said, "Sorry, didn't mean to laugh. Do you think she's been making voodoo effigies and sticking pins in them? Killing us off that way?"

"Something like that," I mumbled.

"I have a few too. I think we all do. It's a coven thing. Nothing sinister, and actually voodoo gets a bad rap. It's not for evil, it's just magic and religion combined."

"So what are the dolls for?" asked Charlie.

"You make them for people you care about. You can focus your magic on that person by holding their effigy. If you have their hair, the magic's even stronger. You can send, and don't laugh, positive vibes their way. Concentrate your energy and try to help them out. Better health, better prosperity, or luck, whatever you want. It's not to make them ill, it's the opposite."

"Oh, wow, that's a relief. We hated to think of her up to no good in her little bungalow. What do you know about red string then?" I wondered, seemingly on a roll here with the newest and seemingly most open coven member.

"Red string? You mean this?" she asked, perplexed, as she pulled out a small bundle from her pocket.

"Yes! Everyone has it, and we think it was used to hurt Clem. We'll explain in a minute, but can you shed some light on this? Why do you have it? Why does everyone?"

"It's the only one they have at the ironmonger's that's worth buying. It's reinforced with something and very strong. But, um, the main reason is that they made a mistake with their ordering and had too much so they lowered the price and were selling these huge rolls really cheap. We bought some for coven stuff and then I think everyone went off and bought a roll for themselves as well. It was such a fab deal, it seemed silly not to. Even Dad bought three rolls, and Clem's got a load of it stored somewhere. When we're doing spells that need it, we use it, or for tying up papers for fire offerings, bundling twigs, that kind of thing. It's just string." Em shrugged, utterly at a loss as to the point of my questions.

"That's it? Okay, great. Now, why don't you make us that cuppa? Then we'll explain what's been going on."

"Sure. You coming too, Harlow?" Em tickled him under the chin and he squirmed with delight and coo-purred again. I'd looked up the noises squirrels made and their meaning, and the coo-purr was what they did around mates or mothers to their kits. Maybe Harlow thought of her as his offspring?

We followed Em down a ridiculously long and wide hallway, gawking at the expensive paintings, the antique furniture, and what were undoubtedly very expensive vases, and into a very modern but surprisingly homely kitchen. It was huge, with a relaxation area comprising a sofa and chairs plus a large TV, but it was the enormous island that was the centrepiece. With a built in hob and sink, there was still enough room for six stools on the other side, and Harlow jumped off Em and sat in the middle, taking in the room.

"Nice kitchen," gushed Charlie, drooling with shiny tap envy.

"Yeah. Mum loves to cook, and Dad's always entertaining clients. It's a bit much, but I know we have it good."

"So your dad's a lawyer?" I asked.

"Guess you heard about that yesterday? I didn't ask him to cause such a fuss. But once he heard I was at the police station, he stormed right down there and demanded they release me and everyone else. He's a stickler for the rules, and knows his business inside out. I don't think the police knew what hit them."

Em smiled at us, clearly a little embarrassed, but didn't try to downplay her fortunate circumstances or pretend it was different to how it was, which many people would in her situation.

"He was looking out for you. That's nice," said Charlie. "What did the detectives ask you?"

"Just the usual, I guess," shrugged Em as she filled up the kettle then switched it on. "Where I was when things happened. What I saw. That kind of thing. There wasn't much to tell, and it was all rather half-hearted actually. They kept getting interrupted, their bosses I guess, and then Dad turned up and he brought me home soon after. Then I heard they'd closed the case. That it was an accident. But it wasn't, was it?"

"It couldn't have been, could it?" I said. "Things like that don't happen. Someone set Aunty Clem up for a fall. They tied string across the stairs so she'd trip, and blew up her attic and killed Sylvester. There was a crystal ball, a very small one, and the police decided that was what killed him. But even before that, they'd insisted it was an accident caused by the explosion. Debris of some kind."

"That make sense." Em busied herself with a cafetiere, then poured us coffee and left milk and sugar out for us to help ourselves. "Why would someone try to hurt her? And is this why you were asking about string?

"Yes, they used it. And the explosion is suspicious. But I also found string in the garden, and the crystal ball. But it wasn't there when everyone first looked, but the police still wanted to put it down as an accident."

"I heard all about Clem and her husband from Dad. He knows everyone, and he said they'd close the case as soon as possible out of a sign of respect. Save her any embarrassment, is what he said. He's seen it before, apparently. They pull out all the stops when someone kills somebody by accident that they want to protect, and shut it down before anyone makes a fuss. Often, it doesn't even get into the papers. It's about who you know."

"That's exactly what we've been finding out. But they're wrong. They have to be. It's tied up with the coven and magic. We're sure of it. I can't think what other explanation there could be. That crystal ball couldn't have sailed over the house."

"It could have bounced. It might have gone flying up high, hit a tree, and hurtled over into the back garden."

"Doubtful. And you know when you just get a feeling?"

"I get them all the time. Like you wouldn't believe," sighed Em.

"Your gift?" asked Charlie.

"One of them, yes."

"That's what we both have. A feeling that there's something else going on. We just haven't been able to find out what."

"But you're trying to?" Em leaned forward, watching us intently, and her long black hair fell over her face. She brushed it aside, keen to watch our reaction.

"We haven't got any choice. If someone's intent on hurting Clem, we need to discover who. And why? Do you trust the others? How well do you know them?"

"I trust them, but with reservations. Does that sound terrible?"

"No, not at all," said Charlie. "Why with reservations?"

"Well, and this is just between us, okay?" We nodded eagerly. "Everyone has secrets, and when you are into this magic and stuff then there are more secrets than ever. We all have our spellbooks, and we share information, but only some. Everyone's looking for the next cool thing, you know? A wicked spell, a way to make a potion that really works, how to get better at reading crystal balls, shortcuts for ramping up your wand, loads of stuff."

"Makes sense," I said.

"I'm the new girl, right? Only been with the coven a few weeks, so I have to prove myself. Especially because I'm so young. Clem and Shirley, even Miranda, are really impressive, and know loads of amazing stuff, so I share most things I know. Not everything, but a lot. And they mostly reciprocate. Clem taught me a few awesome spells, and I'm practising them, but Mike's different. Half the time it's like he doesn't even believe, and the other half he's showing off. But he's very secretive, and doesn't share much, and he's said himself that when he talks to anyone else, he brushes the whole thing off as a joke."

"But that's understandable. We didn't think this was real either," said Charlie.

"That was obvious. It's hard to explain, but Mike is too secretive to be in a coven. He doesn't give as much as he takes, and pretends he doesn't know things when he obviously does. Don't get me wrong, I like him, and he dresses so cool, but there's just something about him."

"We spoke to him and it's definitely a weird set up. And he told us he can't actually do any magic, that it's more of an interest in the occult and things like that."

"How come you guys believe now? What changed?"

"I found a wand with my name on it. Clem made it for me. I used her spellbook and, er, well, it worked. Does it make you tired too?"

"That is beyond cool!" Em's whole face lit up. "And very rare. You must be a natural. I knew it was in the family. Clem told me her and her sister, your mum I guess, were gifted since little girls, but for someone whose never even tried before, well, that's impressive."

"Thanks. And what about you? Do your parents know?"

"Oh yes." Em waved away the notion. "Dad knows, and tries to pretend it isn't real, but Mum's a natural. Not that you'd think it to look at her, and she never, ever speaks about it to anyone else. She doesn't do much, as she's always so busy, but she has the gift. I've always had it. But I'm still learning, and not very good yet. I can do a few basic spells, and I'm good at reading people. Too good, maybe, as I see right through people and I, er, I have this other gift that I absolutely hate, but it comes in handy sometimes."

Charlie and I were practically on the counter now, eager to learn what it was. Harlow edged closer to Em, seemingly just as interested.

"What is it?"

"I can, um, I can see ghosts."

"For real?" asked Charlie, glancing around nervously.

"Yeah. And it sucks. It's not all the time, thankfully. I mean, there aren't any here or anything, and it's not like that show in the old house where the woman sees them everywhere all the time. It's more of a sometimes thing. Now and then I see them, and can even talk to them, but they don't stay for long, and kind of fade in and out of existence. Sorry, it's hard to explain." Em laughed as she rubbed at her cheek, then her face became serious and she said, "We could try with Sylvester, if you'd like. I might be able to talk to him. That's if he's still around. He might have moved on, or maybe not. You can never tell when they will. Some are around for hundreds of years, others never at all."

"That's a great idea," I said. "But only if you're sure?"

"I'm sure. It might be kinda cool. And um, will Young Dave be there?" Em reddened and let her hair fall over her face.

"Young Dave? Yes, he's back there. My Mum arrived earlier, so we do need to get back actually, but yes. Why?" I asked, when her discomfort made it clear why she was interested.

"Nothing. Just wondering. Right, shall we get going then?"

"Don't you need to wait for your mum to get back?" asked Charlie.

"I am eighteen, you know. I'm not a kid. I can do what I want. And besides, they have these things called phones now." Em chuckled as she pulled her phone from her pocket and called her mum to explain she was going out for a while.

We finished our drinks, then Harlow hopped onto Em's shoulder, snuggled down, and we left to go see if Sylvester was still hanging around in spirit form.

Just when I'd thought things couldn't get any weirder.

Chapter 17

Thankfully, Mum was still asleep when we arrived. The last thing we needed was her trying to stop us, or interfering. She might not want anything to do with the supernatural, but the rest of us were more than keen to give this a go.

We found Young Dave taking it easy out in the garden, but the moment he saw us he jumped up from his seat and said, "Hi," awkwardly, before kicking at the paving.

"Any news?" I asked.

"The hospital phoned the landline. They said Clem can be picked up at two. So we've got a few hours yet."

"That's great. Did they say anything else?"

"Nope, that's it." Young Dave turned to Em and said, "How are you after yesterday?"

Em blushed cutely but parted her hair and smiled as she said, "Fine, thank you. It was a shock, but I'm doing okay. What about you?"

"I'm good. It was freaky, but we've been trying to figure it out. So, what are you doing here? Um, not that it isn't brilliant to see you." He grinned awkwardly, and it was evident these two had a thing for each other.

"Lucas and Charlie wanted to see if I could help. I can, er, see ghosts."

"No way! That is so cool!"

"You think?" Em beamed and took a step closer to Young Dave.

"Course. Wish I could do stuff like that. All I can do is paint."

"But you do a great job. I was, um, watching you yesterday and you looked so professional. As if you've been doing it for years."

"Really? Cool. So, you were watching?" he asked, grinning so widely his smile would soon disappear around the back of his head.

"Just a glance. Only to see what you were doing." Em giggled and put her hand over her mouth, then brushed at her hair as she turned sideways a little.

Charlie and I smiled at each other, but this would have to wait as we had more important matters to attend to.

"Em, what do you need? How do you prepare for this?"

"I just need it to be quiet, and I'll go to where he died and see if he's around. But he might not be, and sometimes even if they are, they don't talk. Some are very confused, and others are really annoyed about being dead. But Sylvester was a nice man, so if he's here, I'm sure he'll want to talk to somebody who can see him."

"Okay then. Do your thing."

We watched Em walk down the garden, heavy boots incongruous with the warm weather. I turned to Young Dave and noted the gormless look, his tongue almost lolling out. "Easy there, tiger. Play it cool. And stick your tongue back in."

"She's so amazing. I know she's really hot and way above my level, but do you think she likes me?"

"I know she does. She was asking if you'd be here. I don't know why, but yes, she likes you. Seems like you and me can both charm women way out of our league."

"Don't mess with me, Lucas. I don't want to make a fool of myself. Are you sure? I mean, her folks are rich, and she's so stylish, and so cute. I'm a painter. An apprentice painter," he added, eyebrows dancing around his face.

"Yes, I'm sure. And yes, I'll take you on permanently. You're a great worker, although you need to get better at arriving on time. If you do, the job's yours."

"Yes!" whooped Young Dave, fist-pumping the air.

Em turned and put a finger to her lips, so Young Dave mouthed a silent sorry then beamed at me and whispered, "How should I play this?"

"Just ask her out on a date. Go to the cinema or something."

"We don't do that kind of thing anymore," he frowned. "At least I don't think we do. Maybe I'll ask her what she likes doing? Or, yes, I know, I could take her to see a band. She's into music, so that would be fun."

"Great idea. Now, let's be quiet and watch."

With Young Dave brimming with happiness, I smiled at Charlie and she gave my arm a squeeze, then we watched Em as she stopped at the spot Sylvester had died. Harlow stood between us, eyes focused, then began to chatter quietly as the air shimmered beside Em and for a split second we all saw a spectral form before it vanished.

But seemingly not for Em. She took a step back, let her arms hang limp, then spoke softly so we couldn't hear, but was clearly having a conversation. Every so often she'd shift position, sometimes even looking up, as if the ghost of Sylvester was moving around.

I studied Em closely, noted how she kept her hair from her face, presumably so her expression could be seen, and how her hands were relaxed, but occasionally she would point at things, and once at us, then at the bushes and even at the trees. She frowned for a while, clearly trying to understand, and I think she asked for Sylvester to repeat what he'd said. She nodded, but frowned again, and then smiled. Then she reached out, but her arms suddenly dropped, and she sank to her knees.

"Em!" Young Dave ran forward, and we chased after him, but love makes a young man fast, and he got to Em well before us and held onto her before she fell sideways.

"Are you okay?" I asked as her eyes blinked rapidly several times then opened.

"I... I'm fine," she smiled weakly, then shook her head. "Wow, that was an intense one. It takes it out of you, just like using magic does, but that was exhausting. I'll be fine in a moment. " She smiled at Young Dave and said, "Thanks for looking out for me."

"Of course. You sure you're okay?"

"Yes, thank you."

"You smell nice," Young Dave blurted, then hopped to his feet and stood there, not knowing what to do.

"Thank you. It's perfume," she said, as if that needed explaining.

"Right," said Young Dave, well out of his depth now.

"Let's get you inside so you can sit down," said Charlie, shaking her head at the ineptitude of all men. She helped Em up then we wandered slowly back to the house, Harlow leading the way, chattering excitedly.

Once Em had taken a seat, we joined her at the table and when she was ready, which took several minutes, she said, "That was weird."

"You're telling me," I said. "Ghosts. Can you imagine?"

"Not me," said Charlie.

"So cool," said Young Dave, tongue beginning to loll again.

"He was rather upset, as is understandable, but I calmed him down and he definitely knew he was dead. I think he'd been waiting there. He said he tried to talk to you all but you didn't answer, which upset him, but he hung around hoping I'd come, as he knew about my gift."

"So what did he say?" I asked.

"He was very confused, and often ghosts don't remember much, but he kept talking about seeing a soldier. Something about the war. Think he might have got jumbled up with things. He loved war movies and liked to talk about his grandfather's time as a soldier. Had his medals and everything. I'm not sure, to be honest. But what he did say was that he remembered seeing a ball flying towards him, then he was dead. But he was insistent about a soldier, and there was something vague to do with wood. Like he wanted to fix the attic or something. As I said, it was rather jumbled and he was talking really fast."

"Did he say anything else? Anything at all?" I asked.

"Something about the fence, but he was fading fast then. To be honest, they get like this quite a lot. The last things they see are often what they focus on, and my guess is he was looking at the plants and was focused on the fence and garden and then he died."

"And we've checked the fence repeatedly," I said. "I looked again earlier, and it's just the new panels from last year and the nice plants. There's nothing there. There was the crystal ball, but that's it."

"What a shame," said Charlie. "All that trouble for you and he didn't help us catch the killer."

"At least he's passed on now. He said what he needed to, even if it didn't make much sense, and now he's gone. Oh, one more thing. He did ask about string."

"The string again?" I sighed. "What about it?"

"He asked if it had worked. He seemed confused, and when I told him about Clem tripping, he was genuinely upset. He didn't remember that happening at all."

"But he asked if the string worked? Did he say he put it across the stairs?"

"No, but he seemed genuinely upset when I told him Clem took a tumble. Dunno, that was it." Em shrugged, and her eyes began to close, so we didn't press her for more.

"That's been really helpful. Thank you."

"Are you sure? It doesn't clear much up, does it?"

"Maybe, or maybe not. You never know what suddenly clicks in your head once you have time to mull things over. That's quite a lot to go on, actually. And I get the feeling that once Clem gets home, we're going to learn a whole lot more. You look shattered. Let's get you home, shall we? But there's one thing I think we can be certain of."

"What's that?" Em's eyes began to close again.

"It wasn't you who murdered Sylvester!" shouted Young Dave, then slapped his hand over his mouth and said, "Sorry, I startled you."

"That's okay. I needed a jolt," she laughed.

"Young Dave, why don't you take the van and drop Em home? We'll go and pick Aunty Clem up later in the Mini, so no need to rush back."

"What? Are you sure? You never let me drive. You always said I wasn't to even touch the steering wheel."

"You make me nervous. You haven't been driving for long. This is an exception as Em needs to get home, but we need to be here in case the hospital rings. They were meant to call my phone, not the landline, but I guess things got jumbled up. You youngsters head off. We'll wait here."

"That would be lovely," said Em, smiling at Young Dave.

He practically sprang from his seat, knocked his chair over, righted it, then held out his hand for the keys. They left, chatting excitedly to each other, oblivious to the rest of the world.

"They'll make a sweet couple," said Charlie. "Thank you for being so thoughtful."

"He's a good lad. And she seems nice."

"She does. But what if she isn't really? What if it was her all along and she's been playing us? Maybe Sylvester did something horrible and this was her revenge."

"But we saw the ghost," I spluttered.

"Did we? Or did we see a quick flash of a spectral figure that she conjured using her gifts? What if she's murdering Young Dave right now? You'll have to get another apprentice and start training all over again." Charlie giggled, and I sank into my chair, my heart hammering.

"That was not funny."

"You should have seen your face," Charlie giggled. "No, seriously, Em seems lovely. Very grounded, considering her background. But what a burden that must be. Would you want her gift?"

"No," I shuddered. "I couldn't think of anything worse. Think there are ghosts in the house?" I studied the kitchen, wondering if her gift could somehow rub off on me and I'd turn to find a load of characters from history staring right at me.

"Probably. Although Clem's been here for a long time. So, what did you make of all that?"

"I'm mulling it over. There's something there, but I don't know what. Maybe Sylvester set the trap for Clem, and that's why he was asking if it worked. But then Em said he seemed shocked that she'd hurt herself, so I just don't know. They definitely have a thing about string though. It's weird."

"Everyone loves having a big roll of the stuff. It always comes in handy."

"Do you?"

"Yes. I've had it for years. But it's black, before you ask. I bet you've got loads."

"I do," I admitted. "And come to think of it, Clem did say something to me a while back about a deal on large rolls. I didn't pay much attention because I have plenty, but maybe she was talking about the red stuff."

"Most likely."

"What about this soldier thing? What could that be about?"

"No idea. Maybe he was fixated on his grandfather. Thinking about him because he died in the war. I hate to admit this, but it is seeming more and more likely that he got killed by that crystal ball. It must have been energised by magic for it to do so much damage, but nothing would surprise me anymore."

"I think you might be right. He said as much himself. We've been doing all this chasing around, and now it looks like we've just been making fools of ourselves."

We sat in silence, fed up and feeling a little silly for not believing the police. We got caught up in the adventure of amateur sleuthing and all it had done was cause a lot of upset and stress and done nothing but get us worked up over nothing. It was time to go back to painting walls and the odd bit of handyman work and forget this had ever happened.

But still, something was niggling me. I just didn't know what. And at least these last few days hadn't been entirely fruitless, as now I knew there was magic in the world. Real, actual magic. How cool was that?

Hunger slowly began to gnaw away at me now the adrenaline of the chase had worn off. All I was left with was an empty feeling in the pit of my stomach, and the sense that something still wasn't right, but a concern that I was acting ridiculously.

I made us a lacklustre lunch that did little to fill the void, and we ate mostly in silence, neither of us having much to say beyond a few more conjectures that got us nowhere. We were beat. We'd spoken to everyone we could think of, several people we hadn't considered, and unless we went door to door asking everyone if they'd killed Sylvester, there wasn't much more I could think of to do.

At half one, and with Mum still asleep, we locked up, left her a note, and headed off to see if Clem might be ready to be discharged a little early.

My spirits lifted when we pulled up at the hospital and she was already waiting outside.

"Yes! We don't have to pay for parking," I grinned.

"You cheapskate," laughed Charlie.

"It's not the money. It's the evil machine." I jumped out and beamed as I approached Aunty Clem.

"Lucas! So wonderful to see you."

"You too, Aunty. Why didn't you call if they let you out early? We could have come sooner."

"I didn't want to be any more bother than I already am. And besides, it's been lovely just sitting here and breathing proper air. I felt like I was sucking on a bottle of Domestos in there."

"I know what you mean. Come on, let's get you home."

"Ooh, lovely. Now, what have you been up to? I bet you've both been uncovering this mystery, haven't you?"

"We've been trying to, but it hasn't exactly worked out that way," I said, doleful.

Once in the car, and with Charlie and Clem having had a few words, we set off, and Clem didn't stop talking the whole way. Starved of company apart from the busy nurses, she regaled us with a blow by blow account of the comings and goings of the ward, along with a rather overly lengthy commentary on the state of the NHS in general and how the poor nurses were run off their feet.

Luckily, the trip was short, and we arrived home soon enough. After helping Clem out of the Mini, we stood outside her house and she sighed as she looked at the wrecked frontage. But then she did the oddest thing. She laughed.

"What's so funny?"

"Oh, just the fact my house blew up. But at least I came away unscathed. Well, almost." She glanced at her arm and winced. "The main thing is nobody else got hurt. Apart from poor Sylvester. Such a shame that poor man got killed because of my own stupidity. It didn't seem real until now, but seeing the house like this has brought me to my senses. I feel so guilty."

We both gasped as we turned to stare at her, open-mouthed.

"You what!?" I blurted. "What are you talking about? You didn't kill him. You couldn't have. I was with you the whole time."

"I'm afraid I think I did. In fact, I admit it. I killed Sylvester. I'm so sorry, and I feel terrible to think you youngsters have been running around chasing a murderer, when all the time the killer was me. I'm a wicked woman and I deserve to be punished."

"We better go inside," I sighed, feeling light-headed and sick.

"That's a very good idea," said Charlie, frowning at me and shrugging her shoulders.

I shook my head, not knowing what to say, or what on earth Aunty Clem was talking about.

Chapter 18

As we entered the hallway, Mum came down the stairs, yawning as she tried to straighten her mussed-up hair. She studied each step intently, clearly worried there might be another booby-trap, but when she noticed us, she smiled, and declared, "Clem, you're home!" and with her concerns forgotten, she raced down the remaining stairs and hugged her startled sister tightly.

"My, what a surprise. I wasn't expecting you. What are you doing here?"

"I came to make sure my sister was alright. I caught an overnight flight the moment I heard you had your fall. Are you okay? Does it hurt?" Mum stepped back to study Clem, and pointed at her sling. "That looks nasty. How will you manage with a cast?"

"I'll be fine as long as I keep it wrapped in the sling, and it will heal better. But you really came all this way just for me? And look at you, so pretty, and what a lovely tan. I need to get out in the sunshine more."

"Yes, less study and more relaxing. I suppose now the attic's gone you can find the time to relax."

Clem's face soured as she said, "Please don't start. I know you don't like me studying, and you certainly don't approve of the magic, but I gave it up for so long and I just couldn't find it in me to ignore it any longer."

"Clem, it's okay. I wasn't going to argue about it," said Mum, reaching for her sister and resting her hand gently on her shoulder. "I think maybe it's time I stopped being so silly. You're right, and so are Lucas and Charlie. Magic is a wonderful thing, and we mustn't let what happened ruin it for us. For you. I'm sorry. Can you forgive me? I miss us being close how we used to be. I know it's my fault, but please forgive me."

"Of course I do," sighed Clem as she smiled and reached out to hug Mum with her good arm. "Thank you for coming. It means so much to me. And you truly don't mind about the coven? And the magic?"

"No. It was silly, and I was wrong. I shouldn't let the past bother me so much."

"What happened?" I asked.

"Let's go and have a cuppa, and maybe we can finally put the past to rest," said Clem. "And I do need to explain what's been happening. I'm afraid I did a terrible thing."

"Aunty Clem, I don't know what you're thinking, but this wasn't your fault. The police got it all wrong, they must have. They just bulldozed this without doing a proper job."

"Oh, that's where you are so very wrong," said Clem as she took my mum's hand and they marched into the kitchen, leaving Charlie and me staring at each other in utter confusion.

"What is going on?" asked Charlie.

"I have absolutely no idea, but I think we're about to find out. Have we been idiots?"

"I think we might have been."

At that moment, Young Dave came through the door, whistling and beaming from ear to ear, and Harlow appeared from where he must have been waiting outside.

"Somebody must have had a nice time," I noted, happy for him. "You've been gone ages."

"Em invited me inside. Can you believe it? She even made me a sandwich. They have this huge fridge that talks to you and even gives ice cubes. Imagine. They had this posh cheese and ham to die for, and even chutney her mum made. She made her own chutney." Young Dave shook his head in wonder, like this was the first time he'd ever heard of such a thing, which I guess it was.

"Young Dave, lots of people make their own chutney."

"Well, my folks certainly never have. It was amazing. And guess what?"

"What?" asked Charlie, chuckling.

"They have a pool. A swimming pool. In their house! And Em invited me over tomorrow. Now I need to go buy some swimming trunks. Should I get Speedos or shorts."

"Shorts!" we both blurted, staring at his matchstick legs.

"Right. Um, why are you standing here?"

We filled him in on what had just happened with Clem, and he said, "So you think we've been idiots and somehow she's responsible?"

"I don't see how she could be. But she thinks it's all her fault. Let's go and find out what's been going on. Seems like we've been wasting everyone's time, and our own." I couldn't imagine how this was Aunty's fault, but knew we'd been acting foolish and were about to be shown why.

"She can't be to blame," protested Young Dave. "After all the work we've done. Everything we've found out. Hey, did you know that Em's great with magic. She can do spells and everything." Young Dave smiled again, clearly not going to be depressed by anything now he had a girl in his life.

"Well done for getting on with Em," I said, patting him on the back. "You deserve to have a girlfriend."

"She isn't my girlfriend yet," he laughed. "But I'm working on it." With a smile to each of us, we headed into the kitchen.

"...your fault, Clem. It can't be."

My aunty and Mum both turned when we entered.

"What's up?" I asked.

"I was just explaining to Bee that I don't blame her for not wanting to get involved in magic. I understand." Aunty Clem squeezed Mum's hand and they both smiled at each other.

"And I was saying that I don't blame your aunty for wanting to. It's been such a long time, that her getting involved in it all again just took me by surprise. I know I should have handled it better."

"So, what happened when you two were young?" I asked.

"You know that I'm a little older than Bee?"

"But you wouldn't believe it," said Young Dave, always looking to ingratiate himself so the tea and biscuits kept on coming. "Because you both look so young, I mean. Not that you both look old or anything."

"I'd stop now if I were you," I laughed.

"I think you're right." He bowed his head but his good mood was not to be denied, so added, "Great to see you home, Clem. We looked after the place, though, and had a lot of adventures. And Harlow has been brilliant."

Harlow jumped onto the table and began chattering away, and Aunty Clem leaned forward to study him, clearly interested. Mum watched him, too, and then both women exchanged a knowing nod and smile.

"He's got the gift in him," said Mum.

"He does, Bee," agreed Aunty Clem. "Whatever happened to him?"

"I thought we'd told you?" I said. "Remember, he got knocked unconscious by the explosion. Must have blown him out of the tree."

"Oh no, now it's all making sense," sighed Aunty Clem.

"Are you thinking what I'm thinking?" asked Mum.

"I am. Oh dear, this just gets worse and worse. What am I to do? I'll have to hand myself in to the police. I deserve to be punished. They'll send me to jail and put me away for years. This is all my fault."

"Clem, don't be silly. They've finished their investigation, so it's done. You have nothing to worry about."

"But I couldn't live with myself. I killed poor Sylvester and this is down to me. What a fool I've been. Look at the poor guy." Aunty Clem reached out and ruffled Harlow's soft, red fur. Dust scattered across the table, and both women leaned forward to inspect it then nodded knowingly.

"Yes, it was me alright. I'm so sorry, Harlow. I could have killed you too."

"He was unconscious for a while, then he was fine. He landed on poor Young Dave here, which probably saved his life."

"I'm a great catch," beamed Young Dave.

"And your head's big," I reminded him, lest he forget. "But what are you talking about? How is this your fault? Harlow got hit by the explosion and got that dust from whatever you were making up there and it made him smart or something."

"Not just smart. But magic smart," said Mum. "And it wasn't the explosion that made him so clever, and the potion wouldn't have been potent enough to make him smart if he was in his tree."

"No, it wouldn't," agreed Clem. "So now it all makes sense and I'm a terrible person."

"Will someone please explain what you are talking about?" I sighed, taking a seat after Young Dave and Charlie sank into free chairs.

"I think you better sit down," mumbled Aunty Clem.

"Um, I already have."

"Right, yes, of course. Gosh, what a mess. Has anyone made tea?"

"I'll do it," said Young Dave, jumping to his feet.

"Don't eat all the biscuits," warned Aunty Clem. "I know you always take a few sneaky ones if you make tea."

"What, me?" asked Young Dave, trying to look innocent and failing miserably.

Nobody spoke until Young Dave had made tea, let it steep in the teapot, then poured us each a cup and stuffed the good biscuits into his mouth like he hadn't eaten for weeks.

"Okay, let's start at the beginning. And by that, I mean why exactly did the police basically dismiss the fact the attic blew up, someone tripped you, and a man died?"

"Because I told them to. Or, not told, asked. DI Durham knew my Bill. He was only young back then, an up-and-coming officer, and my Bill looked out for him. He brought him up through the ranks and he thought very highly of us both. I told him what I'd done, and he said he'd deal with it. And to be fair, he did. I should never have let him. People should be punished for their crimes. I think the pain made me act stupidly, but now I see the truth and will have to pay the price."

"He covered up a murder?"

"Not cover it up. He rushed everything through, and so did his bosses, because like you already knew, your uncle was well-respected."

"And what exactly did you tell him? And why didn't you tell us earlier? We've been chasing around speaking to everyone who was here, and finding clues, and you're saying it was all for nothing?"

"I never thought for one minute you'd be so good at it," chuckled Clem. "You three make quite the team of sleuths. You should go into business."

"I just want to paint walls and put up shelves," I sighed.

"So what really happened, Clem?" asked Young Dave, eager and happy despite what we'd been through.

"I thought, and I'd convinced myself of this, that someone was sneaking into the attic and stealing my things. Actually, I'm sure they had. And looking through my spellbook too. That's not allowed. So, I, er, I set a trap. I'm afraid it went horribly wrong."

"A trap?"

"Yes, I made a potion, although really it's more a powder. I set it up so that if anyone touched the lid of the box my spellbook was in, it would go off. The plan was it would cover them in the powder and then I'd know which member of the coven it was."

"Was this a spell you invented?" asked Young Dave, leaning forward, eyes wide.

"Yes, a simple enough thing so that if anyone but me tried to access my private book they'd be covered in the stuff and I'd have my answer."

"And it looks like we found the thief," said Mum, rubbing Harlow's head as he chattered away excitedly.

"Harlow?" I blurted.

"Yes, he must have been coming in through the window, which I always leave open as it gets so stuffy up there, and the fumes get quite nasty if I'm brewing up a particularly strong potion. He must have been trying to access the book, and poking his cute little nose into things he ought not to."

We looked at Harlow, who had the good grace to bow his head and remain silent.

"He was stealing things? That's why there were so many weird items at the base of the tree? They fell out when the attic exploded?" I asked.

"I suppose so," said Clem. "Harlow must have triggered the trap and I, er, must have got the spell or the powders wrong, or mixed up or something, and it worked a little too well. It was meant to make a loud noise so I'd be able to confront the thief, but it did much more than that."

"It's a tricky one to master," said Mum, full of sympathy.

"Harlow, were you taking things from the attic? Did you make the explosion happen?" Harlow looked up and grunted once. "Thanks for being honest." I turned to Aunty Clem. "So, you set the spell and it caused the explosion?"

"A bit of an oopsie," she said, smiling.

"Yes, a very big oopsie."

"But one good thing has come of it. I'm going to get double glazing so the window won't need painting."

"No, but I still have to paint the whole front of the house again," I grumbled.

"This time I'll pay. I know you're busy."

"Young Dave can do it. He likes going up ladders."

"Does he?"

"No, he hates it. But he's got younger legs, and longer ones, so he won't mind."

"I will," grumbled Young Dave.

"Let's talk about your fall next. Someone set you up for that, so how can that be your fault?"

Aunty Clem blushed as she fidgeted with her empty cup of tea and said, "I set it."

"You didn't!" shouted Charlie. "Whatever for? And if you did, why would you trip on it?"

"I forgot," mumbled Clem.

"Clem, you silly woman. Whatever were you thinking?" asked Mum.

"I got caught up in the moment. I set the spell and the potion, but then I thought what if that didn't work? So I decided to add in a little something extra. I almost made myself sick banging nails into my beautiful stairs, but I only used little ones and figured I could get you, Lucas, to fix the damage once I'd taken them out."

"You set it yourself? That's crazy."

"I was rather overzealous, I admit. I wanted to figure out who the sneak was, and thought that if they tripped, and it would only be onto the half landing, then I'd know for sure. It was my backup. I put the nails in early in the morning, then when I left the others to go to the attic, I took the opportunity to put the string in place. Only problem being, I was so excited about the coven meeting that when I came back down after going to get my Tarot from the attic, I forgot it was there and tripped over it. I took the string out quickly, but had to leave a nail. The other one came out when I fell, so I hid that away and hoped you wouldn't notice. But you did. And that's where the trouble started."

"I can't believe I'm hearing this. That was very foolish, and very dangerous. You hurt yourself."

"I regret it so much. I caused so much upset and heartache, and this isn't even the worst of it. I killed Sylvester."

"You didn't, did you? Don't tell me you set a crystal ball to explode at someone in the garden?"

"No, don't be ridiculous. As if I would do that! But I told DI Durham what I'd done when we spoke, and he understood. I didn't say anything about real magic, of course, but I told him I'd set a trap with chemicals to give someone a scare and it must have gone wrong, and I told him about the string."

"That's why he was so dismissive of it," I said to Charlie.

"It makes sense. He tried to convince us it had always been there."

"Like I said, he owed my Bill a lot. He was just looking out for me."

"And now we get to Sylvester. How did you do it?"

Clem frowned, then asked, "How did I kill him?"

"Yes. You said you did it."

"I honestly have no idea how it happened. But DI Durham said there was no other explanation, and when he came back after you found the crystal ball that was the end of that. Actually, even before that, he'd convinced everyone it was because of the second explosion. The crystal ball must have hit the tree, and with all the magic around it must have bounced over the house and killed poor Sylvester."

"At least you didn't booby-trap him," I muttered.

"I would never hurt anyone like that!"

"You tried to blow someone up in your attic and trip them down the stairs!" I shouted. "What were you thinking?"

"I got carried away," mumbled Clem.

"It's alright, Clem, you didn't do any of it on purpose," said Mum.

"She just said she did. It's totally irresponsible."

"But at least nobody got hurt," said Young Dave through a mouthful of biscuit. We all turned to stare at him. "What?"

"Someone did get hurt, Young Dave. Aunty Clem did, Harlow did, and so did Sylvester. In the words of Mike, Sylvester got made super dead."

"And I'm to blame. I should go down to the station now and hand myself in."

"Don't be silly," said Mum.

"I don't think there's any point," I sighed. "It was an accident. An unfortunate one, but an accident. These things happen."

"Do they?" asked Aunty Clem brightly.

"No, they do not! People do not blow up their own attics, make squirrels incredibly smart, and trip themselves on the stairs. They certainly don't kill people with crystal balls." I stood up and rubbed at my temples, then said, "I need some air." I wandered out into the hallway for some reason, rather than going out into the rear garden.

With a shrug, I opened the front door and went outside, my mind reeling with everything Aunty Clem had admitted. Halfway down the front garden, I was distracted by the sight of something that finally made me understand exactly how Sylvester had really died. It was obvious, and had been staring me in the face the whole time.

"It was you!" I shouted, then started running.

Chapter 19

Joe, Aunty Clem's next-door neighbour, stopped dead in his tracks, arms laden with his battle reenactment gear. His eyes went wide, his tanned face turned incredibly pale, then he panicked, and dropped everything. As he ran back into his house, swords, chainmail, and even a beautifully made shield clattered to the driveway. I raced down Clem's garden, turned left, and stormed up Joe's drive.

"What's going on?" shouted Charlie as she and the others appeared.

"It was him. Joe," I shouted over the low hedge that divided the properties.

"What was him?" asked Mum.

"He killed Sylvester. It all just clicked into place." I banged on his front door and shouted, "We know you're in there. Come out and face the music, you assassin."

The others came and joined me while I continued hammering on the door to no avail.

"Lucas, what's got into you?" asked Charlie.

"Don't you get it? It's been staring us in the face this whole time. It was Joe. He killed Sylvester."

"Whatever are you talking about?" asked Clem. "We know how he died. It was the explosion and the crystal ball."

"No, it wasn't. We never should have gone along with that nonsense. The garden was checked and the crystal ball wasn't there. Someone planted it."

"It was an oversight, nothing more," said Clem softly, trying to calm me down.

"You're wrong. He put it there. Joe's the murderer."

"What makes you so sure?" asked Young Dave, looking worried.

"I bet it's still out there. Come on, I'll show you." I opened the letterbox and shouted through, "There's no escape, Joe. I'm going to prove it to everyone. You should have owned up."

"Go away," shouted Joe from somewhere inside the house. "You're scaring me. I'll call the police."

"Go right ahead. I bet they'll want to hear about what you did." I let the letterbox snap shut and told everyone, "Follow me."

Before I began to second-guess myself, I stormed around the side of the house and opened the gate he hadn't had the chance to lock because he'd been retrieving his reenactment gear. Keen to ensure I wasn't losing my marbles, I raced across the manicured lawn and partway down the garden where I approximated the crystal ball had been found on Clem's side.

As everyone caught up with me, I said, "See? I knew it!"

"What are you talking about?" asked Charlie. "It's just his garden and the fence."

"Yes, but look. It's obvious from this side. I thought it looked different from Clem's, but assumed it was just the plants blocking the sun from the fence panel so it hadn't faded as much as the others. The panel is new. He replaced it. Where's the old one?" I glanced around the large garden, then spied the panel poking out from behind the workshop he used to store some of his reenactment equipment and where he was forever making new pieces. Joe was not only a carpenter by profession, but a skilled metalworker and an avid collector of memorabilia.

I dragged out the fence panel and as everyone gathered around, I said, "Look at the hole. The panel was smashed when Sylvester was killed. And then Joe switched it. He had a few left over from when he replaced the fence last year. I remember him telling Aunty Clem about it."

"That's right, he did. And the panel does look different from this side. But what does this mean? You're saying Joe killed Sylvester, but I don't understand."

I left the panel and searched around the outside of the workshop, but couldn't find what I was looking for. Knowing I was right, but that I needed proof, I flung open the unlocked doors. Inside were benches full of materials, half-finished weapons, with racks covering the walls.

A thick green tarp was what caught my eye, so I raced over then pulled it off to reveal what I should have remembered when this first happened.

"A cannon!" gushed Young Dave. "Cool. He's got a cannon."

"I remember him telling me about it last year when he was doing the fencing. Said he'd picked it up at an auction for next to nothing and he was going to restore it once he found the time. Well, he found the time alright, and then he hid it away after he killed Sylvester."

"Lucas, you're acting crazy!" said Charlie. "Why on earth would Joe kill Sylvester with a cannon of all things."

"Let's let him explain. But I'm right, I know I am. It all slots into place now. He broke the panel when he fired the cannon, so replaced it when we were gone. Nobody noticed because Clem's garden is so dense with plants, but it would have been seen soon enough so he switched the panels and hid the murder weapon."

"A cannon?" asked Mum. "Who kills people with cannons? Joe wouldn't do that. And he wouldn't do it in the middle of the day."

"He did it. And he hasn't had the chance to get rid of the evidence yet. I bet he was going to move it today for his reenactment battle tomorrow. Let's go and get him."

We exited the workshop, then paused when Joe came trailing down the garden, head hung, eyes darting in every direction but at us. He looked like a broken, defeated man, but nobody spoke until he stopped in front of us.

"Joe, this can't be true, can it?" asked Aunty Clem softly. "Lucas thinks you broke the fence panel then replaced it so you wouldn't be found out. You didn't really kill poor Sylvester with your old cannon, did you?"

Joe lifted his head and wiped the sweat from his forehead. He nodded, mute.

"That is so cool," said Young Dave, shaking his head in wonder. "Not that Sylvester's dead, but that you have a cannon. You didn't do it, did you?"

"I'm sorry. I'm so sorry. I panicked and didn't know what else to do. The police came so soon and then left so quick and everything happened so fast that I told them I didn't hear a thing because I had my headphones on, but I didn't. When everyone left, I replaced the fence panel and was amazed nobody had noticed it. Then I just rolled the cannon back into the workshop. I was going to tell, but then it was done and I panicked. I rubbed the crystal ball in the grass where Sylvester died then dropped it by the fence, thinking that might work, then when you found it the problem was all over. I've been feeling just awful, but I don't want to go to jail. It was an accident. I promise it was. I just didn't know what I should do."

"You should have admitted the truth," I said. "You killed someone and you should have owned up. You planted evidence and tried to hide what you'd done."

"Joe, how could you?" said Aunty Clem. "And why? What a horrid thing to do."

"It was just an accident. I got carried away. I never even meant to fire it. But I'd finished repairing it, and it looked so amazing. I wondered if I could test it out. I loaded the cannonball and, er, packed the gunpowder, just to be authentic, as it really is a rare find."

"Yes, just get on with it," snapped Clem.

"Sorry, yes. Well, you know I prefer my reenactments to be as realistic as possible, and I always do things properly. I'd loaded the powder into it, and I, er, I might have lit the linstock. Not to actually set it off, you understand, but just so I could picture myself on the battlefield about to fire a real cannon at the approaching army. Next thing I knew, there was this almighty explosion. It was your attic exploding. That was a shock, and I, er, I forgot what I was holding. As I was standing there, listening, everyone came out into the garden. I was distracted, and then I must have dropped the live end of the linstock into the touch-hole where the powder was and it just went off. Nearly took my foot off with the recoil as it shot backwards at me, and then all hell broke loose. There was a hole in the fence, and in Sylvester too, and then everyone was shouting and screaming and I didn't know what was happening."

"So you hid it?" I asked.

"I did. I'm so sorry. I fixed the fence as soon as I could, and as an afterthought later I planted the crystal ball. My mind was addled, I couldn't think straight. My belly hurt so bad and I knew it was wrong, but I did it anyway. It was silly, and I should have put the crystal ball somewhere else, but I thought the panel looked just like the others. I wasn't thinking straight. I wanted to own up, but then it was over with and I figured it was best to stay quiet. It was an accident. I swear it was. Please forgive me. You'll never guess how far the cannonball travelled. It was right at the bottom of the woods. I searched for ages. And it was only small. Imagine the damage a large one would do. I could blow up a house." We stared at him, aghast. "Not that I want to, of course."

"But it caused so much damage. Do cannonballs do that?" asked Mum.

"They do," said Joe keenly. "In fact, they can travel through more than one person. And even when they bounce they can cause terrible injuries."

"And you stuck a cannonball in a working cannon, stuffed it with gunpowder, and lit the fuse," I asked, incredulous.

"It isn't a fuse. It's called linstock. You light that then touch it to the gunpowder."

"Sounds like a fuse to me. And I don't need a lesson on cannon terminology," I snapped. "What on earth possessed you to do that?"

"I was just seeing if it worked properly. If the cannonball fit and if I'd done a proper job repairing it. Seventeenth century models like this are very rare. I was just excited."

"And very stupid," said Aunty Clem.

"I know. And I'm sorry."

"Can I have a go?" asked Young Dave.

We turned to him and shouted, "No!" before he got any more bad ideas.

"What happens now?" asked Joe.

"Now you have to own up. And I expect a lot of people will be in plenty of trouble besides you," I said.

"Why would anyone else be in trouble?" asked Aunty Clem.

"It's a bit of an oversight, don't you think? A cannon, and they didn't think to check for gunpowder residue or anything on poor Sylvester."

"Why would they? Nobody would think it was a cannon. I mean, who would?" asked Aunty Clem.

"True," I admitted.

"Will you help me?" asked Joe, shoulders hunched, kicking at the grass as he looked at me.

"Me? What can I do?"

"Maybe have a word with the police. You seemed pretty chummy with that detective. I heard you talking when you found the crystal ball."

"We are not chummy. This is one problem you're going to have to deal with yourself."

"Will I go to jail?"

"They'll understand," said Aunty Clem, waving away any notion of this being serious.

"Of course they will," said Mum. "Accidents happen," she added breezily.

"Mum, he killed someone. With a cannon!" I shouted, exasperated.

"Only a little one," said Joe brightly, clinging to this last vestige of hope.

"There you go then," said Mum, patting Joe on the back. "It was just a little cannon."

"Oh, well that's all right then," I sighed. "Joe, you need to call the police and tell them what you've done."

"Will you do it? Phone that detective maybe?"

Everyone turned to me, so with a shrug I said, "Fine, but no trying to escape," I warned.

"Where would I go?"

"I have no idea. To be honest, I just want to go and have a lie down."

I pulled out my phone, then paused as there was an almighty crash from the workshop. Harlow came bounding out, chattering wildly, then launched at me and sat on my shoulder as a black ball rolled out of the open doorway and stopped between my legs.

"Yours, I presume?" I asked.

"Er, yes. That's a smart squirrel. I thought I'd hidden it well."

"Was this what did it?" asked Young Dave.

"Yes, that's the one," groaned Joe. "See, it's only little."

I stroked Harlow and congratulated him, then dialled the number for DI Durham.

After a very brief phone call in which I explained little beyond that we were currently with the person who murdered Sylvester, I hung up after he promised to be here in ten minutes or less. After explaining to everyone that DI Durham did not sound like a happy detective in the slightest, we stood there, unsure what to do.

"What happens now?" asked Young Dave.

"I guess we should all go back to mine," said Aunty Clem. "We could have a cup of tea."

"That sounds lovely," cooed Mum.

"Aren't you both a bit freaked out?" I asked.

They frowned at me, then Mum said, "No. It was an accident. Joe didn't do it on purpose. These things happen."

"Will you stop saying that? They do not happen."

"It did this time," smirked Young Dave.

"Yes, I suppose it did. Actually, tea might be nice."

"Can I have two sugars?" asked Joe. "It might be the last proper cuppa I get if I'm going to be locked up."

"Yes, and I'll even get out the good biscuits," said Aunty Clem.

"Ooh, what a treat," said Joe with a grin.

Charlie and I shook our heads at each other, then trailed after everyone as they chatted away like we hadn't just confronted a man who'd killed someone with a cannon.

At Aunty Clem's, we hung out in the kitchen while she made tea, then ate good biscuits until twenty minutes later DI

Durham arrived looking flustered, angry, confused, and interested all at the same time.

Everyone tried to explain what happened at once, until he silenced us all and left Joe to talk. He spoke fast, left nothing out as he always did love the sound of his own voice, and when he'd finished admitting his crime, DI Durham just slumped into a chair and groaned.

Aunty Clem gave him a cup of tea and the last few biscuits, which cheered him up a little, then when he'd recovered enough from the shock he read Joe his rights and took him away.

"Mum? Aunty Clem?"

"Yes dear?" asked Mum.

"What happened when you were young that turned you so against using your gifts?"

Both women exchanged a glance, then Aunty Clem nodded to Mum. "There isn't much to tell. It was just an accident. We were young, and silly, and very excited about what we were discovering. It all went horribly wrong, and we vowed never to use magic again."

"Did you kill someone?" asked Young Dave, eyes wide. "There's a lot of it about at the moment."

"Kill someone?" chuckled Mum. "Of course not. Nothing like that."

"Oh. I assumed you had," I admitted.

"No, it was much worse than that," said Aunty Clem.

All eyes were on them as Mum drained her tea and said, "We lost our puppy." Her eyes welled up and she pulled a tissue from her shorts pocket and sniffled.

"It was a terrible thing."

"Did you kill it?" I asked softly.

"Oh no. Mr. Snuffles was right as rain. But he vanished for over half an hour and we were frantic. We were both bawling our eyes out until he suddenly appeared. Except..."

"What?" we all asked.

"He wasn't a puppy anymore. He was fully grown. Mum and Dad were so angry with us, and we got into a lot of trouble. We missed out on him growing up, so there and then we promised never to do anything with our gifts ever again."

"And I'm sorry I started again," said Clem. "Look at all the trouble its caused. I should have known better."

"This wasn't your fault," said Mum. "Er, at least not all of it. But no more booby-traps, and no more powders and potions in the attic."

"I won't," said Clem, nodding eagerly.

"Sorry about the puppy," I said. "That must have been awful."

"It was, but I'm sorry too," said Mum. "I should have told you that you had the gift. You could have been learning all these years, but instead it's taken this horrible incident to show you the truth."

"And Aunty Clem? How come you made me a wand? I like it, and thank you, but why?"

"Because I knew Bee would come around eventually," she chuckled. "And I knew you'd be a believer soon enough. Do you want to learn how to use your gift? Is that okay, Bee?"

"Of course. He's a grown man. He can make his own decisions."

I turned to Charlie, who smiled as she shrugged and said, "It's up to you. But as long as you don't go trying to make me or Young Dave disappear and we come back years older, then I think it's great."

"Me too," said Young Dave. "I can't believe you're going to be a wizard."

"I am not going to be a wizard," I pouted.

"You are," goaded Young Dave. "A wizard detective."

Harlow chatted excitedly and danced around on the table, causing everyone to laugh.

"This has been a long few days," I sighed. "Magic and murder. Who would have thought?"

"But you solved the crystal ball conundrum, and that was very smart," said Aunty Clem, beaming at me.

"I think Harlow solved more than I did. He led us to all the clues. And, actually, most of the clues turned out to be nothing of the sort. You lot are definitely obsessed with red string."

"It was on offer! A once in a lifetime deal. You can't miss out on prices like that," said Aunty Clem. "Now, does anyone know the phone number for a good roofer? I don't think Joe's going to be able to do it any time soon."

THE END

I send out emails when new books are published, so please sign up for news about releases and sales. No spam. Just book updates. Promise.

Printed in Great Britain
by Amazon

41368577R00108